COMES A TIME

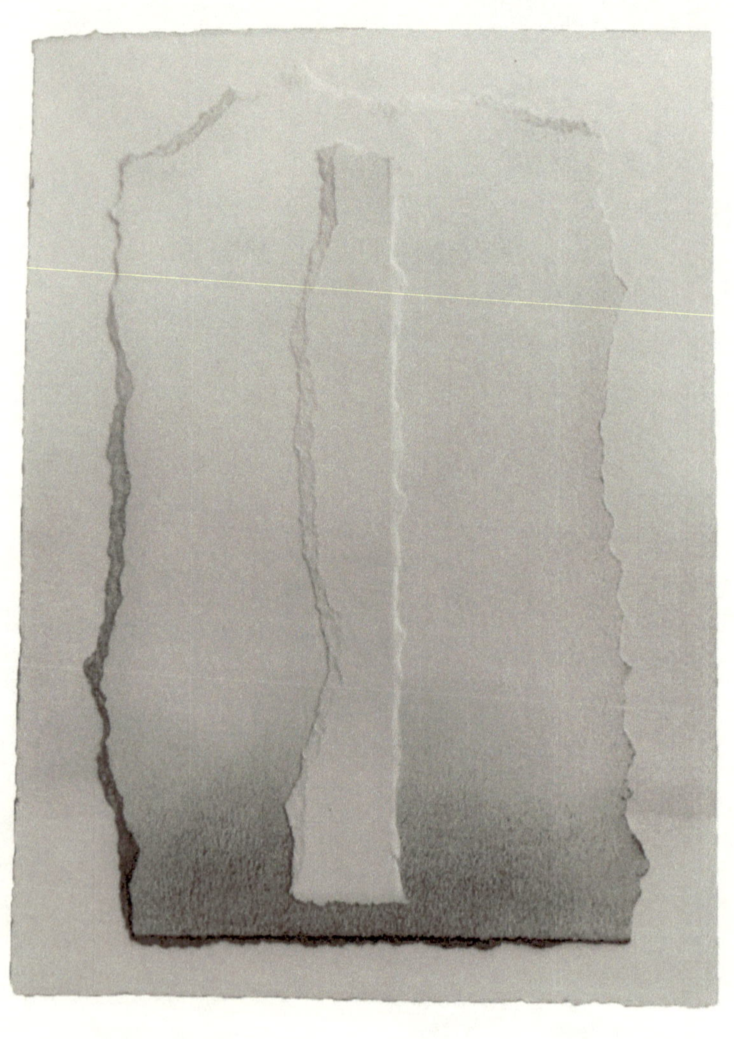

COMES A TIME

Frederick Ramey

Fomite
Burlington, VT

ISBN-13: 978-1-944388-72-0
Library of Congress Control Number: 2018967929
Fomite
58 Peru Street
Burlington, VT 05401

for R.A.R.

My bones are a family in their tent
huddled over a small fire
waiting for the uncertain signal
to resume the long march.

Stanley Kunitz
"Day of Foreboding"

The Waiting Place

Nov__ sm 2 O - DAY

Undbl You st fos t fin

mebnow -

THE HANDWRITING DIDN'T LOOK LIKE HIS. Neither did the hand. It was so thin. And it was shaking just a little bit. Not like the aspen leaves. Are there still leaves now, so late in the year? He looked down the cold mountain to see and then raised his arm to follow the slope. It was shaking just a little, that hand, like it was afraid, and it was spotted and pale and turned in a sad way. Because it was old. That was something Raymond understood well enough.

He gathered his great coat around him and moved his legs to warm them, or maybe just to be sure where they were. Then he nestled his back, trying to fit the flat rocks a little better, used his hat to pillow his head.

That pen's a good one, he thought, looking down at it. But he couldn't call the brand just then. He knew it was a pricey one that didn't skip much; reliable. He had always written well with it, he thought. Letters and orders and checks every month, like watch work. It felt good and thick in the hand. And it was marbled, green and gold. He smiled a little to find that word — *marbled* — because it surprised him. Raymond had gotten the pen sometime before he could remember, probably after the war, when he was working for Fluorin Construction. He could remember *that* — and he wondered why he could, when there was so much he couldn't call. Then he remembered that old Lacey had passed on a few weeks, or really years ago, so that Raymond didn't know anybody there anymore. At Fluorin. He'd heard it from somebody that Lacey was gone, and once, he thought, there had been a pencil that went with that pen. Probably still in that desk at the house, there in the middle . . . box . . . in the shallow . . . the pullout. The shallow *drawer*— that's what it's called. And *shallow* is as good as *marbled*, even when *drawer* won't come up at first. Good when any word at all comes back as itself, really. Anymore.

They did that still from time to time, the words. At least early in the day like it was. But numbers were a problem since he'd had all this trouble. He thought he could still write words, if that old hand would — in fact, he already had. See here? — *Undoubtedly, you set folks to find me by now.* He'd brought pens along. They'd been in that old satchel. Must have been for some reason.

Raymond studied the wide sheets he'd written on. They were still open on his lap. And he tried to think what the book was. It seemed to him the size of those jordans that children use, children at church. No that wasn't right. Children at school, yes. But then he realized the pages were green and that there were pink lines, both side to side and up and down, or however you spell it. Just a few of them. And so he knew the sheets were for numbers. It was *that* kind of jor— . . . Well, not like Vic's. But Raymond wouldn't be writing numbers down. Those were words on the page already. So he could write words still, just like he thought — though they looked a little odd to him. Maybe it was that green paper.

Raymond's words changed sometimes now between the moment he thought them and the moment later when they tried to come from his mouth, changed like they'd been cooked. Or changed in the way bugs become other bugs. It was strange, and sometimes it frightened him how that happened. But the changes also seemed to him like some natural, hidden process, the kind that had always caused him to wonder and that seemed even more mysterious now.

If he separated himself from the people around him — even from his boy Raymond — no, David; *Raymond* was Raymond. If he didn't worry about whether they understood him, those people, then the words that changed before they came out of his mouth were like dark butterflies over a field. A misty sort of field, really. They were just something that didn't belong to him. And sometimes, when he wasn't frightened and when he knew where he was, they could seem beautiful to him — like butterflies and like reading poems that a fellow couldn't quite understand the first time through.

Raymond used to do that — read poems. Vic had taught him to do that. Vic was his father. Raymond was Raymond. And then there was that David boy.

But if he was going to write words on those green and striped pages, he'd have to be careful. Or what he wrote wouldn't make any sense. He'd have to let the changelings go. Let them fly out over that field, until the right words came, words that hadn't changed. Then he could put those ones down on the page. And he knew there wasn't much time. It had taken him a long while to read that note and fix that old satchel to his shoulder so it rode pretty good. He remembered. And he would be cold soon, when the soul went down and it was nigh time.

It would probably be the last nigh.

Raymond moved the marbled pen in his fingers, rolled it like a smoking car. He shook his head. Like a cigar he'd meant.

Undbl You st fos t fin
mebnow —
Im hih throks an they waus eme
Thas wha I wait

Good. He looked around just to see what else he had brought with him, but then he saw everything there. The dirt beneath his legs was almost white, and all the plants nearby were dry and winter dead. Though it must only be fall, seemed like. There were little brown leaves where the stones beside him met the dirt. Above, he could hear the long blow in the trees. He meant the wind. When he looked up he saw that the tree limbs were like some bony structure beneath skin that wasn't there. Something that maybe he wasn't meant to see, some hard lines that made shapes possible. Whenever there was shape. His hand hardly seemed like a hand anymore. But the trees did.

It was better sometimes if he didn't try to call the names of things.

Raymond had once been possible. He once could walk over mountains. And he could carry things in both hands. But today, it had taken him hours to climb up so far from where that orange car — or a blue one — had dropped him. He remembered that driver who took all the money he had and then drove away in a cloud. Of course, that was what the driver was supposed to do. That's what was planned in the note. And now Raymond was high up in rocks, where he could see like little David in a tree. See to the very ends maybe, and far away from everyone.

There hadn't been much in the satchel, he remembered. It hadn't included the things he would have liked to bring with him, but only very little, like the water. They were all important things, he was sure, or they wouldn't have been in there. He knew to believe in the man who wrote the note and packed most of what was in that satchel. The list of things Raymond was supposed to add to when the time came. But none of that included the things that had memory attached to them — none of them did, except the pen, which had been his for a long time. It was green and gold all mixed up. Oh, he had his cane with him, too, and the satchel with a strap that had fit over his head and shoulder and had scrunched up all bulky and painful behind him on the car ride over. And what he was supposed to bring was all folded up inside it. That satchel. So that Raymond deLeone, waiting, could think about who he had been.

1

NOT TOO MANY DAYS BEFORE, when the sun shone through the wide kitchen window at the back of the house, Raymond could still tell the time of day. Though he couldn't always call the numbers for the hour anymore or even the name for the — the moon . . . that is, the mano — the . . . first part of the day. Within him were words like "crescent" and "nigh" and "sleep." But there was more in there than just those simple ones — and it was this, really, that confused him. It didn't make sense anymore that he knew "wine dark." He thought it meant blue, even though he'd have trouble saying it out loud. And it was strange to him that he could somehow remember that "a kelson of the Creation is love." He had begun to catch phrases like that in his head, phrases he'd read a long time before, and words he didn't normally use — like that "kelson." He wasn't at all sure what that meant.

But the deLeones were memorizers. Always had been from the first preacher among them. That was just the truth of it. And a while back, when he began to see that he was going to suffer the same wordlessness his father, Vic, had gone through, Raymond had thought it might be valuable to focus on what he could still remember. He thought that if he opened some of Vic's old books in that back room and reminded himself of the verses Vic had taught him when he was young, maybe, just maybe, it would stave off all this trouble. He thought it would be like waking a child with touches and whispers. Something like that — a complex kind of waiting on his own words like on a sleeping child. There's warmth in that.

All of which was to say that he was still Raymond deLeone inside his mind, whole and well set in space, if not quite in time anymore. He understood that. Inside him, the words ran like colors through his silences, connecting without much difficulty to his memories. It was only that very often they couldn't make the path to his lips or to the things in his hands. Sometimes he couldn't name what was right in front of him, even though the thing might be haloed in his memory by all that had come before, all that was behind it. In his glass of water, there by the kitchen window, he saw himself lifting glasses with Clara, in nightclubs and restaurants and at the kitchen table with their little David. The slip taste of fish — he liked fish — *that* taste would run over into a hot afternoon in California when Clara's hair was so thick he couldn't move his hands through it without pushing her head back so that her salt-white throat came bare to his mouth.

Nothing was itself anymore, really. And all of it was like stacked sheets of glass. To Raymond the daylight moved from all directions at once. The pictures he could see were pretty clear he guessed, but they were too radiant ever to be called by a single word.

Radiant. That's the awe — all, he meant.

A cup of coffee was the sounds she made moving through the kitchen. That Clara. A piece of paper, if he moved it, was her voice when she whispered. For some lost reason, the smell of the high woods reminded him of kisses. The sound of a car made him think of being alone first with her and then too quickly without her, really — it was Clara's being gone whenever he heard a car start, the times she'd left him, and the final leaving that every year was now. Seemed like. The white rushing of mountain water called all the doors he had shushed closed behind him — he'd climbed alongside that kind of water on his way up to these rocks.

And just shrugging into his suit coat was like taking Clara into his arms, her breast so full that it was a solace beyond the reach of words. A fellow takes on responsibility with a woman like that, really.

But he'd failed that somehow so that as the glass pictures of his remembering faded out, his Clara became in eff — or unfull of … something.

In the long ago days when Raymond had been trim and a little threadbare in his secondhand coats, back when he still carried whole poems in his head, he had found her in the green grocer across the street from the office where she worked. There wasn't much promise in life in those years, but that made the need for nearness greater in him. And so he watched her, taking his lunches when she did, building his days around the hours she came and went. And, from a distance, he saw that she was always accompanied by other women and that she walked with her arms tucked tightly, with one hand in a jacket or skirt pocket, the other crossed horizontal before her. The little purse in the crook of that elbow, he knew, was only an excuse to keep her arm between her womb and the world.

She almost never smiled out on the street. She probably thought that would be unseemly. And so she'd set her eyes on the middle distance and pull whatever friend to her through those cocked elbows, her hat tightly pinned against the press of that hair. Sure there was worry in everybody's eyes in those days, but the fear seemed darker in her somehow, as though she knew more about limits than the other girls did — or maybe just more about losing. He couldn't tell, but he knew that her sadness was attractive to him. It looked to be a kind of melancholy that was all at once lighter and deeper than his own; he could see that, even from across the street — sadness behind so bright a troubled face. He was drawn to it as to the melting mood that drink brought on in him. And that's how he came to know what longing was, really — from all those days looking at Clara with a drink or two behind his tongue.

Before he spoke to her, he had conspired to take a couple of her friends to the motion pictures or to dinner, friends he had seen on her arm. He could do that then, talk to women, approach them unannounced, persuade them to walk with him, to sit down and smile for him. And he had listened to each one of them talk for hours about how nice that one night going out with him was or about the dreams they had for making a home. In those days women didn't ever presume, but that one future was all they ever talked to a fellow about. It was in their whispers to him over little round tables with dull linens and tiny electric lamps, and in what they said to him as they sipped their coffees and highballs.

It was Ellen who had told him the most.

In those years, all the rooms in the city were marked by pools of light that made people lean toward one another like that. But then, maybe what caused the leaning was just the war. Outside, in the summer months, you could still lie in the grass under that vast, bright Colorado sky and imagine something endless. But inside it was different.

Vic had taught him that what is endless requires endurance, which wasn't necessarily what Raymond wanted. In those days he wasn't much interested in what might come from a long way out. He was too young for that, and the girls he passed on the streets and in the markets and along those stone hallways all looked and smelled to him of a closer release than any future could promise. And a deeper, more enjoyable one, he was sure.

Now, even those pool-lit places were gone, and out on the streets the trees had mostly been cut down. The walkways downtown were cleared of tables and wrought iron. And so everything moved faster in the city these days. But back then, when he realized the girls would say whatever he wanted to hear without seeming to wonder why, he began to ask them about her, about Clara and her sweet unhidden sorrow. They told him her people were farmers.

Settling again against the high rocks, Raymond crossed his legs at the ankles like a young man, which made him chuckle. They could dance a lick, those tailor cuffs. That's right. But they're old now, he thought. Old like that hand.

Clara's parents had been farm people they told him. And so she knew what staying was. But they were already gone by the day he first saw her. Alone, she'd had no way to hold on to the farm, and so it had been auctioned off one cold morning a few months before. On the next Monday, first thing, she had settled all her father's accounts, as far as the thin cash would allow her to, and boarded a bus to the city. It hadn't been far to travel, but it was a great deal too far ever to go back. Denver was still a slow city in those days, a city that didn't see itself as part of anything greater than the high plains to the east and the mountains that stopped it from being part of the desert west. A few miners still showed their rugged selves in the city back then, and the railway through the Platte River side of downtown still carried cattle. From the middle of that old city, a quiet girl could almost hear her home in the rustling fields a hundred miles northeast. Almost, but not quite.

Clara hadn't come to Denver after some dream but only for the work, and because she'd had no other choice. It was just where she had to be, and so she was always sure she was out of place. Raymond had figured that was what had caused her to come down so perfectly to a point when she walked, especially when she wore that big-shouldered jacket, when she wouldn't turn her head from the way she was going.

The girls at the round white tables talked on until Raymond knew some of what troubled Clara, knew how to avoid all that, how to assure her, how to approach her so that her head would turn. And then his own life had come clear to him. Or he thought it had, the scrim of some imagined future with a wife and some surety. And so he'd crossed Fifteenth Street one afternoon when Clara had Ellen beside her, and he asked to be introduced. Since it was lunchtime, he had offered them both oranges from a brown bag and had looked to see whether Clara smiled at them.

Of course, she didn't.

"No thank you," she said with the formality a young woman brings with her into the city. Ellen had looked at him sideways. He remembered that. And she'd smiled, all sly at him the way she was.

He had walked on with them to the five and dime where they were going for lunch, and he talked all the way there, gesturing with the oranges. He could see that Ellen was studying — no doubt remembering how he had spoken quietly with her over those long evenings and wondering if Clara had always been his real purpose. But he kept talking, even with Ellen there, though he had little idea what he was saying, until finally Clara agreed to meet him after work in the tea room at the Denver Dry — that is, if Ellen would come along. For some reason Ellen had agreed, and he had called that just fine and tipped his hat as they left him there on the sidewalk.

When he turned away, all full of himself, he had bumped into the sort of matron you still saw in the shopping districts in those days, older women with vast bosoms and long, thin coats, women of apparent substance despite the hard times. He had apologized grandly, touching his hat again. Then he had given her Clara's orange and ushered her along her way with a wave of his arm. He'd been happy in that moment, foolish and full the kind of grand gesture that sticks to a young man's thoughts of himself. Waving that threadbare arm . . .

Thas wha I wait

yse an Im not lost

last rly

Im not last

The months that followed were the brightest in his life, especially those rare moments in which he made Clara laugh. She loved most, it seemed, his stories about his high school days, back in the Valley. She loved to hear about him running that thief down with his lineman buddy — what was his name? — running too slow behind. Hogue? And about his childhood brush with Bonnie and Clyde. He'd been in the store when they walked in. Old Hancock had recognized them both somehow. And so Clyde had pulled him by the elbow from behind the counter and ushered him outside to the car. They gave him a ride out of town far enough to keep him from talking to anybody for a long while. They let him go then, to walk back with his story while they sped on eastward back to Texas or Oklahoma or maybe Kansas. He'd tell those stories and Clara would tuck her head. When she laughed, she would lower her eyes and fiddle with her handkerchief or whatever else she might have in her hands.

She blushed easy, Clara did. And in those days he thought it was shyness. But it was another flush that colored her when he would take her arm at the door or lay his hand on hers in those pools of restaurant light.

She kept Ellen with them as often as she could, made excuses, worried Ellen's being alone, or just assumed she was welcome to come along so that they were three whenever Clara could finagle it. And that was most of the time.

He took them both out whenever he could, more than

once to the Trocadero ballroom. Those were the nights he remembered most clearly, when his two women would dress to the nines, so high colored that watching them he could hardly breathe. All evening long, they'd lean together like flowers in a vase and put him to tests so that he'd have to look away just to keep his dignity. Especially Ellen and her moonlit tongue.

The two of them would shop all Saturday morning at the Denver Dry, buying lipstick, he figured, and what all. And then they'd spend the afternoon in Ellen's place, doing what he couldn't imagine — but clearly, from the looks of them, spending a good bit of it stacking their hair and shaping their eyes, choosing outfits that always seemed to compete with one another. Ellen would dare Clara to bare her shoulders for the evening, she said. But whenever he went to pick them up, they would meet him at the door wearing those short little jackets over their wide dresses — jackets that just covered their breasts, and with dark lace at the wrists. Once, on a late summer night, Clara had worn a shawl. He had smiled his best and called them gorgeous and they had laughed as if he had no idea.

That night at the Trocadero, they'd had too much to drink, really. Or at least he had. But he remembered sitting at their table, watching the two of them dance — because by then he was too unsteady. First, they danced close and serious, four-steps, making fun of the night, their necks glistening in that odd ballroom light. And then, when he lifted his last glass to them, they raised their eyebrows in answer and began to spin for him with the room and the music, their arms out wide to him and to everything that Clara had never imagined before, everything Ellen had demanded and expected, and everything Raymond deLeone could ever want. He'd never seen her quite so free of herself before that dance.

When laughing is so rare in a woman, a fellow holds on to the memory.

Over that summer, he learned that Clara hadn't read much and that she slept through motion pictures, especially sad ones. She wouldn't eat fish or green vegetables. She was afraid of horses and snakes. And of bridges — she wouldn't walk across a bridge for anything, and she'd ride over one only with her hands wrenched to something solid and her eyes closed tight. But her mind moved quickly enough. She just wasn't likely to say what she thought. And numbers came so naturally to Clara back then that she could account for every cent in the week past and reckon the long-term impact of every purchase. Maybe none of that came to much, but her job was as secure as anyone's.

For all his questions and all that her friends had told him, Raymond still had trouble ferreting out the real cause of her sadness, much less the reasons for her fears. Even Ellen said she didn't understand it all. He knew from the first that they rose from more than just her lost home and her old parents gone, but Clara's sadness was finally unspeakable — at least, beyond the wrinkle between her hazel eyes.

He'd run his finger down that deepening line from time to time trying to smooth it away, which always failed. And she would shake her head at that.

"You can't quiet a bird, Raymond," she'd say. So simply. But in those days he thought different.

"Sure you can, baby," he'd answer her and lay his palms onto the stones of her thin hips. "It just takes two hands."

She'd slap one of them away playfully then. But she would let the other one guide her the way he wanted her to go. And so he looked for every chance to touch her, like a hound that paws what he doesn't quite recognize. Until soon, instead of guiding her, Raymond began heeling to her, letting himself be led the way a woman can lead a man, by the short leash of his need to understand her. They went to the city parks and for long walks through Capitol Hill. And on the day she folded him in with that arm, close enough that she could still lay her hand flat upon her belly, he knew she would marry him. And so he asked her.

She hadn't actually answered — at least not by saying anything. But she had opened her mouth slightly beneath her troubled eyes and had not said no. She reached out and took his hand, when he thought it should have been the other way around, and she pulled him to her so that they could embrace right there in the park and he could, for the first time, taste the depth of her hunger and know that this was the reason for her blush. He was sure that she had moaned high and brief inside the hollow of his opened mouth. It was a sound he thought he had heard, not with his ears, but in the vibrating of his own wishes so that it came from her and from him at once. Raymond had opened his eyes then and seen that the line of her sadness was blushed nearly red.

He pulled back from her and, before she opened her eyes, he touched it again and found it warm.

"You put off heat, Clara."

"Yes," she said, "I do."

They had spent the next month together. And looking back he had come to realize that it was the only constant time they ever knew. For the rest of his life it surprised him to remember that on several mornings in each of those weeks, Clara awoke next to him. When the light of those sunrises would raise him, too, he would open his eyes to find her lying there perfectly still, on her side, watching him, so close by that it took a few moments for his eyes to focus on her. He knew full well that the look on her face in those moments was not love. She seemed instead to be watching him with simple country interest, and — for those short awakening minutes, before anything had been said by either of them, before the day had even made itself real — Clara seemed perfectly calm and safe, even though his arms were not yet around her.

Raymond had known women, but before those scattered mornings none had ever been in his bed when the sun rose. And so at first he didn't know what to think. He would ponder the improbability of Clara for awhile and then smile at her, having no idea what a man should say at such a time. She always smiled back, slightly, and after a moment or two. He probably said something at last, something foolish or funny, or stylish if he could, and then he would need to touch her lightly, to lift the weight of the morning off of them both. And so he would tickle her or jostle the bed, jump up and proclaim himself happy — do something like that. He forced all that broad silliness, of course, but it always made both of them laugh out loud. And sometimes just the physics of it all would arouse them again, despite what he thought were his intentions. That lasted only a month or so, but he didn't think he'd ever been so joyful again.

Eventually, they would dress. He remembered always asking her to wear this or that, because already her clothes had begun to accumulate next to his in that room. She wore the perfume he had picked out for her, and she knew the lipstick he best liked to see her in. She asked him to teach her to tie his necktie, and he had let her do that for him each of those mornings so that he felt a little as though her mark was on him all day long. He would reach up and jerk at that knot from time to time during those days whenever he recalled that he had begun with her beside him.

And he always touched her hair before they left those cramped rooms, just so his hand could remember that part of her, too. Then he'd take her to a hurried, sometimes even walking, breakfast of coffee and toast or oranges as he escorted her to that Fifteenth Street office. Her breakfast remained in the little bag. He was always leaning forward, jutting out his backside and his lips to sip the coffee as they walked — fearful of staining his only suit. And she chuckled at the sight of him like that — a memory that, all these years later, made Raymond smile at the fall mountain sky.

His own work back then, selling ads for the *News*, put him on the streets almost all day. And so he could juggle his appointments to see her sometimes during her break, touch her elbow, maybe tell her a quick story in the hope that she would laugh for him. And whenever he could, whether they had begun together or not, he would take her to lunch somewhere so that their legs could touch beneath a table in the middle of the day.

Raymond knocked his skinny thighs together beneath that great coat and took a deep breath trying to remember the smell of her. Then he exhaled slowly through his wide open mouth to see if it was getting any colder. Seeing the fog of his still being alive, he remembered that in those days they had smoked. Somewhere in that house down there was an old glossy black-and-white photograph of the two of them at a table somewhere or other, smiling over their stemmed glasses. Clara leaning on both elbows, her mouth rounded in shiny black lipstick, her teeth perfectly white, a pillar of smoke rising like a promise from the cigarette in his left hand.

There used to be men in hats with big, popping cameras who roamed those restaurants and on the streets outside, men who would take a fellow's picture without asking and then hand him a card with an address and a scribbled number on it. A few hours later — or the next day or so — you could stop by some nearby studio over one of the plainer shops and get a copy of the photograph. Just to remember that woman on your arm, Raymond thought.

"If you needed to," he said out loud.

But then he guessed that after a certain number of years a fellow *would* need to, even if she still lived with him. And his old face wrinkled up a bit around the eyes, trying to remember what restaurant they'd taken that one picture in. Then he wondered where it might have gotten to.

Raymond was surprised when he realized that Ellen had faded away from them during those first weeks. He had already grown used to having her around them, sharp and steady as she was. She was funny, too, Ellen was. And she had always seemed to him to be the breeze that kept Clara moving. Her golden hair and that sly smile, the way her eyes would widen to mock surprise when he was trying hardest to be modern. And he liked that she was small, coming up just past his shoulder it seemed like. Ellen was slim and certain and forgiving and always the happiest of them all. For the rest of his life with her, Clara seemed to know how much they both needed that one friend, no matter what — her smart advice, her narrow waist and her flaring skirts, the chirrup of a greeting she made whenever she entered their home unbidden, which she did so often that sometimes the air in the house was charged with her.

But during those first weeks Ellen left them alone. And when he realized that Clara hadn't bothered to address her absence, Raymond knew that for his new fiancée it had all been a question of intention. Clara must have known hers, and he had made his own clear by asking her to marry him. He remembered again that doing so had opened something inside of Clara — something more than her lap, though he shouldn't think about her that way. It was as though the nature of her had changed — although what it became wasn't any more available to his calling it than her first nature had been. It was as though she were a vane that had swung about and pointed toward him — and by doing so had made his movement toward her visible. In those first weeks, he felt like warm air moving quickly.

Raymond puckered his lips and ballooned his cheeks out to become the wind atop that one mountain. Another bit of silliness, he thought — and silliness is better than drink, really. Certainly safer — and the thought of safety amused him all over again.

Less than a week before they were married, there came a letter from Vic, filled with news of the changing season and his musings on the war. Although he allowed that the Pacific half was probably unavoidable, he never thought much of it, because Vic wasn't a vengeful man. The letter probably had a few quotations in it, too — the kind that always seemed Vic had chosen at random. But all Raymond could remember was the last line of that letter:

"They've been looking for you awhile," it said.

Folded up inside was an envelope, official and obvious and addressed to Raymond Victor deLeone. Who else would ever call him that but the government? And just that quickly, he was drafted.

Six weeks later, Clara followed him to California, even though she'd never been anywhere before. Not that Raymond had either, really. At first they couldn't be together much, which he had thought made a difference in the immediacy of their life. Even when the flush of their first kiss was fresh in his memory, he'd had the thought that Clara gave herself up to him so hungry because, like everybody else in the world in those days, she believed the war would take her man away. He'd always thought that was why she shared his bed so early. And after the notice arrived, her hunger rose up even higher so that the wind of it was like a hurricane. Maybe it *was* because of the war — everyone said such things. But as high as it reached, Clara's hunger also seemed to him too deep in her to be new born, even warborn. It was a hunger no man would have expected in such a sad and quiet woman, no matter what he knew of her — a need that brought her to anchor against the anguish that rode beside it.

And it was worse, really, because Ellen wasn't with her.

All at once, there in California, he saw that she had been embracing herself when she walked alone on the Denver streets and that she had pressed Ellen's arm to her breast when they were together there. That was hunger, too, he saw. It was her real fear, he figured, making itself visible — fear that he would go and that then she would have nobody. And he saw, too, that the way she pulled him to her was a demand.

She began to feed herself on him without thinking, in the tight, off-base rooms the Navy had allowed them. She came to him with a desire so strong that he felt his own substance, maybe for the first time. When she wrapped him within her at night and in the early hours before he had to report, he no longer knew where he was or what he wanted. And then, a moment or an hour later, when she breathed in short and sharp and high, he would find himself again, just there, in the place that he could barely reach. And he knew himself to be real and full of purpose. But somehow he knew he was also in danger.

Each time, when they finished with one another, he knew that they still were incomplete. Clara would let all the breath flow out of her then and would lie still, heavy and sinking, on her back. Raymond would lay his hand open on the hard, dark mound that rose at her center and let it shape his palm as though it were the bone from which he had just been made. In those long minutes, her heavy breast would fall against him and her hair would become the drape behind which he could confess every wish he had for them together — not knowing whether any wish was really possible. There were new ones each night. And even when he didn't intend it, his need to speak into her like that would raise her hunger again and again until their nights were as full as his days had suddenly become.

Shall we go downtown?

It felt as though he had been finally shaped in those weeks with her, far from her home and from his, in the hot danger of her unspeakable fears. And he soon had trouble remembering a time before he met her. He forgot everything and everyone else for those few weeks, because he had to focus on the threat of her loving him.

But in the days before he shipped out, he saw that her focus was already moving away from him, to the middle distance again, even at their most intimate moments. And he began to see that she was holding on to him for a different reason. She wanted to anchor to him because *she* was leaving — not because he was.

Clara had learned that her hunger wasn't enough. He could see that in the way she'd begun to fold in on herself. Or maybe it was his limitations in satisfying her that had quieted her. That was something he'd never know. But he knew for certain that her heart was slipping from that bare, temporary home near the California base. Maybe it was heading back to the safety of Ellen, or to what had been her father's fields in eastern Colorado. Maybe even past that somewhere. He could see the lost look in her eyes all mixed up with the worries he knew about and those he only sensed. And he understood that the whirlwind of her desire was older than either her expectation or her homesickness.

All that was exhausting to Raymond, and he was having trouble making sense of it. When the muh . . . the mud . . . m-mountain day came back into focus, he squinted at the bare reality of it and raised his arm back up to match the slope — to orient himself. Then he lost the thought all of a sudden, even the desire for the thought, and began turning his hand over and over again to see if there was sunlight there. Such losses happened to Raymond all the time these days. The turning ached a little in the chill air, but it was an easy enough pain, really.

2

Vic deLeone's hands had been small, and the tips of them had been hardened flat by the strings of the guitar he played nights on the porch of their southern Colorado house when Raymond was coming up. Vic sang a little, too. Passably. But it was the squeak and ring of the guitar that Raymond remembered, and the smallness of his father's hands that sometimes had to stretch themselves so wide that his elbows flew up away from him to get to the notes he wanted. Vic was also a tinkerer, and so a teacher, laying his hand on Raymond's to angle a chisel or measure the force of his son's pull, his hand not much bigger than the child's but dry and rough, with ripples across the back like in a shallow pool through which Raymond could see tiny brown pebbles.

From time to time, most often when they were hunting near the river, Vic's hand would lie on Raymond's shoulder, the size of a bird but heavy enough to hold his son still. And they would wait until some movement in a cottonwood along the bosque would catch Vic's eye where he must have seen it before. Then he'd squeeze Raymond's shoulder a bit, bend down to lower his own and point from alongside his son's head to the place where the squirrel had presented, Vic's arm in the position his son's rifle should take. In the long moment before Raymond was willing to raise into the aim, he took strength from the warmth and the sour Prince Albert smell of his father's sleeve. And he'd press his ear lightly against that arm so that he knew not just his father's smell, but how his lanky body sounded.

"You boy," Vic would say, "move slow now, but hurry."

Over. No, up above Raymond now, the cracks in the high rocks were filled with fro . . . with ice, some of them. In those places, the lines were grey. And where there wasn't any . . . ice, the lines were black. At certain places he thought they curved into pictures that were shaded in from roe to brown. The blow rose up now and then, and Raymond's cheeks burned with it. He felt the cold between the fingers in that old hand and saw the pen shaking. He tried again to read the words in the book on his legs, but trying made one eye close in the cold air, and so he turned back up to the pictures on the stones. All his days with Clara, which were moving through him all jumbled together in these last months, were wordless like the picture rocks and the clouds that were clouds above them.

"That's how I know," he said out loud.

He worried a little what to call the colors, but he remembered that the pen was *marbled*. And that quieted him some, so that he was able to steady the pen against the paper again.

Here I catch a spell, he wrote for some reason. Then he reached into the satchel for the water he knew perfectly well was there. The perfectly well water. And Raymond understood that reaching into that bag would stop him for a little while from trying to give the memories names. He didn't have to spell his stories, he thought. Not like he did in those days when he was losing Vic. How-he-felt had never needed calling after that. What he saw in his mind now was more spelling than spelled. Calling names and casting spells, he thought, and he shifted his shoulders against the rocks he'd chosen for this last night.

"That's how I know," he said again, nodding sharply, believing in all those pictures that called themselves up. He knew that they were in his mind. They weren't really in front of him. But he could tell what all he was losing, too.

That David boy didn't think he knew, but he did. That's why he was up here, really.

Then he laid the pen in the center of the book and worked that hand to open the water bottle. But the hand was cold. There should have been gloves, he said to himself. Should have been. Then he thought to twist against the seal with his teeth, to bite down a measure on the circle of it. And when the bottle opened, he took a long pull from its clear neck.

"Cra-royal," he said just as a last wish, almost laughing, and then he thought that maybe what he was drinking just might *be* some whiskey or other. His taste was so dull since all this trouble. But the bottle was clear in that old hand, and it had a little plastic belt ticked to the top that matched it. The swallow had gone down clear, too, he thought and closed his eyes. Just water.

In that glowing private darkness, he was less lost and less there: cold and aching against that ledge. He uncrossed his ankles and banged the balls of his walking boots together, rocking his feet smoothly back and forth on their heels. Though they weren't his old rough-outs, they sounded solid, he thought —made by the mallet.

Im not last.
Hre 1 ctch s pel

It looked as though he'd scratched something out on the green page, but he didn't know when.

He had been twenty years old when he left Vic in that house and moved to Denver. Not left, really. Vic had pretty much sent him out, thinking it was past time. It seemed he could see that his son had the kind of ambitions that farmland wasn't set to meet, even though Raymond still wasn't sure that was right.

He'd been sitting in one of the rusted yard chairs in back of the house all those years ago, thinking about nothing he could ever recall, just facing the railroad tracks above the river a couple of miles toward the Sangres. He'd heard Vic come up slow behind him and could smell the smoke smell of his father before he'd said a word.

"The thing men used to do, as I understand it—"Vic began.

Raymond moved a little in the chair to let his father know he was listening.

"—is they'd head out to the hills somewhere and find a rock sizeable enough not to travel on its own and settin' in a place a fellow could find again when he was ready to. Big enough to stay put." Vic settled into the other chair — there'd only ever been the two of them. Raymond remembered that the chairs always creaked like an old truck pulling out of a wash.

Vic had pulled his Prince Albert out of that sagging jacket pocket, and his rolling papers from the breast and had set to them, while Raymond waited and wondered what had brought this on.

After a time, his father ran both ends of the cigarette in and out of his circled lips and snapped the tin shut.

"As I understand it," he went on, "a fellow would lever that rock up with a stob or some such and then lay in under it a piece of paper or I guess a hide, or some other thing he'd written his name out on."

Raymond had heard the scratch and flare of Vic's match and smelled the burning sulfur and then the tobacco smoke.

"It would be the name his father had given him. Not the name he wanted to be known by just then, but the name that tied him to family." Vic inhaled slow and deep. "Not the name he planned to fill in for himself," he said.

Raymond turned to look at his father, but Vic kept his face to the mountains and exhaled a blue-grey cloud like a solid consideration. Then he spit a tobacco tick off the tip of his tongue.

"That name needed to be kept safe," he said. "And hid away. So the fellow would let that stone down on the name he planned to come back for and then he'd turn toward home. To say his good-byes. You see," Vic finally faced his son, "that would happen when a fellow was ready to go on."

After a long moment, when maybe he thought Raymond would say something, Vic had pushed himself up to standing, stretched his back out, and turned toward the house. Then he'd laid his hand on Raymond's shoulder once more and said. "Denver's just far enough away, son. And I've got a little bit saved up so you don't starve the first week or so."

Raymond had watched as Vic walked away from him, still talking. When his father had reached the back stairs, Raymond finally called out to him.

"Vic?" And his father had stopped and turned back.

But Raymond didn't know what to ask. So his father spoke.

"You don't have the gift to be happy at home any more, son. We both know that."

Raymond may have nodded.

"Would you be all right?" he'd finally asked, admitting something to them both.

"Sons are meant to leave," Vic had said with a quick nod that didn't quite mean yes. "Keeps the house airy."

Raymond had left inside a week, with a half-empty Gladstone and the twenty-eight dollars his father had given him. Out on the front porch, Vic had cradled his son's jaw in that small and hard right hand, nowhere near as old as Raymond's was now, his thumb under Raymond's left eye and his fingers curled toward the back of his neck. And then Vic had lifted his own chin, pointing with it toward the road. Sett Hancock was waiting in the truck at the end of the drive. Sett was going to Denver to make a pick up for his dad's store. It was a long run, but they'd just had to change a tire once, somewhere north of Pueblo. It went smooth enough that Sett had let Raymond off in downtown Denver just after nightfall — the spread of one day, and he had started all over in a place where nobody knew him.

Not much could be better than that.

The wind moved lower and circled him at the thought of starting over, and Raymond gathered the great coat up around his neck. Then, despite himself, he barked a laugh out to the slope — mostly just to see if it would echo. And then he barked again, quick and high but making the sound rattle his throat before letting it go. And he thought that furry little ears must have pricked up all around him, which made him chuckle into the cave of his chest.

"Comes a time to keep still," he said to the rocks.

Raymond didn't like to think about the Pacific War they had put him in except to say that it seemed to him like a contradiction in terms. That's what he'd always said whenever anyone asked him about it, as if it had just been words, when really it had been the opposite. There was a lot he couldn't say about those days, and more he'd promised not to. With all the strangeness of his changing status, Raymond had been gone for thirty-two months, with a single leave in San Diego, where he had spent seven days — and a weekend in Los Angeles — with Clara and her wanting. She'd stayed there to wait for him, far as she had ever been from home and as far as she would ever be, really — until those dry clusters of weeks some years later, when he didn't know where she'd gone.

She waited there, but never wrote to him when he was at sea. The other fellows had girls and wives, too — but theirs seemed to offer up the kind of certainty a fellow could carry into a firestorm, not that such a thing would make a difference really, except in how that fellow felt when he was safe enough to think about it. The girls in those snapshots and letters were all proper ladies in waiting. It was easy to imagine and believe that some day they would open their arms to welcome a fellow home from the wars. And that's what the boys did.

But Clara didn't write — except for a few postcards with California pictures on them and a line or two about where she'd bought them. It was as if she had responded in just the opposite way to the threat of the war. She saw it as a threat to *her*, really — it had left her to survive alone, or it seemed that way from her silence. That was what changed Raymond in the war. Her essential silence. It had taken most of the silliness out of him and very nearly stopped him from talking. He couldn't say anything about it to his buddies. They wouldn't know what to say back and would just move farther away from him.

But Vic had written to him regularly during his tour of duty — those great long letters of his, full of description and accountings and quotations from the books he'd always kept on the table beside his reading chair. That's why Raymond came to reading, because Vic had. It was why he did most of the things he did.

Nestling his old back against the cold st . . . stones, Raymond thought he would give anything to remember those letters — for just one of them to be there in the folded what, the . . .satchel, he'd meant. He reached over and opened it up, that satchel — looked inside to be sure there wasn't one in there — one of Vic's letters. Or maybe the old notebook Vic had given him when he shipped out. He wondered where they all were, those letters, if he'd even saved them. They had been whole sheaves of paper that barely fit into the envelopes his father had licked and sealed with a mouth that smelled of tobacco. They were all twisted and frayed when they finally reached him on the sea, every one of them. They took longer to find him when those transfers started. He could still see the locking circles and horizons of red ink from the routing stamps.

There was so much he hadn't told Vic about those months. About the times he wasn't on a ship but moving in secret through nights that didn't smell like any night he'd ever known. He'd promised not to tell. Sworn it, really, a whole world ago.

Infinite space.

Raymond remembered that from one letter or maybe that his father had said it. That was it. Not what he had read, but what Vic had said. Near the end.

"How'd you sleep, Vic?"

"King of infinite space—" the thin shape in the bed had said to him half the time.

"Vic," he would answer the old, transparent man who had been his father, "It's Raymond." But by then Vic hadn't known who he was.

By the time his war was over, Clara had moved back to Denver and given hard birth to a son they'd named David. They'd almost lost her at that birth, which undoubtedly had changed something inside her. But she had held on and produced a light-haired boy who didn't stop or listen and seemed all the time to be looking for something even as he saw everything. Raymond had tried to understand that about the boy, tried to understand believing there's something else to be found out beyond what's right in front of you — tried to believe for a while like that

David boy always did. Raymond wanted to remember what it was like to be that age, that three and four and five, and how Vic had been with *him* at that time. He wanted to remember so that he'd know what to do and say to make David boy sure that his father would be there if he ever looked back.

But David didn't do much of that. Instead, he watched out for what was far ahead of him — out on some horizon — and ran in lines that you could trace on the grass with a straightedge, ran till he hit the fence or was brought up short by a tree. Then he'd angle off and start again — running and hollering as though he'd burst if he stood still. Raymond would laugh out loud at that. But when he'd check to see if Clara was feeling what he did at such explosions in so small a son, he always found her gone. If she was there at all, she was standing still just inside the back door, maybe watching David, but maybe not, her mouth always slightly open, her arms layered across her belly, a little rounder then than when they had married.

And in all that, Raymond finally saw what his being gone had seeded in her, what her having the boy alone had done. And then her putting eighteen months into raising the boy without him. It had forced her to admit she was alone.

When he came back from the seas, the shadow she walked under was darker. And, God help him, it was more deeply interesting to him. He hated to think that, but it was interesting. He had spent the weeks the world gave him after the war to gather himself sitting under that cottonwood, looking out at his son and back at his wife, almost always with a cold, amber drink in his hand.

Hour after hour, he'd marveled at them and done his best not to analyze it too much — glad he was alive, really, whoever those two people were. Just then, that wasn't too important to him. It was just interesting that the woman he'd come home to was that beautiful and that unfathomable.

"Clara," he would say into her hair. Having come up behind her, he'd lay his hand at her waist, and at his touch and the breath of her name she would inhale deep and slow, her chin rising. Then her spine would turn a little liquid, and the flesh of her would mold itself to his own and slowly move against him, so slowly and privately that he imagined the world away from them and dove into her shadows. Without a word to the boy they would be gone, to their room, and quickly together, sometimes still with her back to him. All from only saying her name to the back of her head. And all that she would reply in those breathing minutes was the name he'd brought home from the Pacific. Ray the Lion — a name he couldn't ever live up to, at least not enough to keep her, but a name he loved to hear on her breath.

She would wrap something around her then and pass back out to where the boy was still playing in his pen or had fallen asleep in the quiet. When he was that young, David was never afraid of being alone, never needed his parents like other children seemed to. But Clara would go to check on him anyway, leaving Raymond without words or other answers, giving him time to realize that she had shown him the darkness in her again.

"You think we still ought to be in this place, Ray?" she'd said to him once, her hands curled around a cold coffee cup.

"I don't know what you mean, darling." He knew there'd been a curiosity in his voice that was too bright for what she was thinking, but he couldn't help it. He'd passed on by her like there was nothing too important in this talking and stepped into the kitchen to get a cup of coffee he didn't really want.

"I mean we haven't either one gone too far from where we started," she said after him.

"The Philippines sure *seemed* like a long ways," he'd called from the kitchen, his hands flat on the counter, trying to put a light in his voice. "A lot closer to water than Colorado, anyway."

"But then you came back."

"That's what sailors do when wars are over."

"Some of them."

He'd turned his head toward the daylight, out the kitchen window where he imagined David must be digging in that sand pile — contouring it, digging to find what he was sure would be treasure, even if it was just his own toys, buried there the day before.

"It just doesn't seem like I'm in the right place all the time, Ray. Do you know what I mean?"

"All right, Clara," he'd said and drawn his breath. He took his own cup in and the coffee carafe to refill hers. Then he sat down at the table with her, knowing that it was this idea of home she was always troubling. He'd learned that about her, too — that except when they were making love, homeless was what she felt. He called it her Out Of place. To Clara, home was always someplace else. Not the farmhouse she'd had to leave when she was still a child, really. Not the rooms in San Diego that he thought about at least once a day. And not this house here, the one her son was growing up in. Clara's home was just some other, imagined place, always out of reach and probably not real. And he could see that it had begun to make her restless, but she acted as though she was all out of hopes.

"So what do you want, darling?" he had asked her then, knowing all of a sudden that they were at a new door. "You want to move? You want another house?"

He knew even then that men are fools.

"I don't know, Raymond," she'd said and then smiled at him, pretending it was over. "Maybe that's all it is."

But he knew that what she wanted wasn't a place that was anywhere. It wasn't a place at all.

"Maybe that's all it is," Raymond said out loud to the mountain and shook his head, though he wasn't sure why, except that it felt good to rub the back of his head against his cap that way, scratching without lifting his arms. Then he wanted to write something else down, afraid that too much t . . . ty . . . time would pass without his making a . . . a mark, which would be a waste, he thought. It would be better if the men who found him could see that he'd been thinking, all the way through. So he picked up the pen, the *marbled* pen, and began to turn it in the light to see if he could tell where it started and ended, be sure it really was the pen and figure which was the business end. He couldn't always trust his feel anymore. When he thought it might be aligned right in that old hand, he put its point to the green paper and watched as a black dot began to expand there, like a hole approaching him very slowly from very far away. Then Raymond forgot what it was that he'd meant to write down. Forgot, really, what he'd meant to do.

"Might just as well . . ." he said to himself and let that hand relax on the jor . . . the jer. That wasn't right, that jordan. Sounded like a name, but not anyone's he knew. He just meant that b . . . bull, book.

"Can't even call it right here in my . . ." Disgusted with himself, Raymond pulled his cap back onto his head with the palm of his left hand. He knew his voice had trailed off into the cold. But he knew, too, that it didn't matter. Never did when he was alone, which didn't keep him from being embarrassed, even standing there in the middle of his bedroom, before his own chest o' drawers. That's it, *drawers*. Ray the Lion laughed once through his cold nose.

He'd told Vic way back then that Clara was always talking about being in the wrong place and that he worried that David would hear her talking that way and get scared. Everybody worried about what the children were feeling in those days — a brand new thought that came out of books and experts. There were child-rearing experts back then who hadn't lived through life but only studied it. And what those experts said had made people whisper and use the wrong words, big ones they thought the kids wouldn't know. It was as if they were talking not to be understood, so that it seemed to Raymond, even then, that nobody quite made sense anymore.

Although Vic still did back then.

"I don't know if I can keep her, Vic," he'd said into that heavy black phone. Raymond had closed the door in his office and turned to face the window. "I sure as hell can't keep her happy." He could just see his father on the other end of the line, standing at the phone niche in the dark hallway a day's drive south, one knee cocked, his small free hand running over and over through his hair.

"Can't *ever* be sure of that, son. Not with any woman."

Ray had sighed deep with knowing. "That's not what I mean, Vic. This isn't like that."

"It's always like that, son, even when times are pretty good — maybe especially with a woman like Clara. She was a sad one when you met her. You knew that."

Yes, he'd known that. It was what he liked most about her, really, that and the way she felt warm in his hands.

"So what do I do?" he asked the phone.

"Just address the sad part, I guess," Vic had said, as if there were a way to do that with a woman like Clara. "Maybe you ought to send David down here to visit for a few weeks. Be good for you two to be alone again for a while."

"How do I do that, Vic?"

"Do what?"

"Address the sad part."

"Oh, that." Over the phone, Raymond could hear his father's lips part from around his cigarette, hear the long exhale. He could almost smell it.

"I think you do that mostly by touch, son," Vic had answered with a smile in his voice.

But Raymond already knew — just as Clara did — that, however powerful touch was in her emotional rivers, it wasn't the answer. Still and all, they did as Vic suggested. They tried. Some of the nights in those weeks were dear to Raymond all right, and the force of some moments remembered might have been sweeter than anything he ever experienced again — maybe more than the nights before they were married. It was as if those nights had left marks on his body.

"You just need to let me," she would whisper into his neck, and then she would drift away and say things that were cut clean from the mooring of the room and the conversation and from him.

"Well," she would sigh. "It goes without saying."

At first he thought she was joking.

And then it began to seem as though even her night-time embraces — her reaching and nibbling and taking him in

— were nothing more than a way for her to hold on. Not necessarily to him, but to any anchor she could find. And when they were spent, he and Clara, there in the cherry-wood four-poster, she would draw away from him so that she was no longer still and open upon her back as she had been when they first married. And he could see her sadness spread out and shadow over her curled body like another blanket.

The only time she wasn't that painfully sad was when she was with Ellen.

"That's the way," Raymond said to the chill mountain air.

Ellen came by almost every Saturday, and Clara would laugh once, high and true, whenever she heard her friend chirrup through the front door. Then they'd chatter at each other — like in a foreign language — for a while before pecking David and Raymond goodbye. Then they'd be gone. Ellen would take Clara shopping and out to lunch. Sometimes they'd go to City Park, they said, and ride the boats. There was a bathhouse on West Colfax, too, where they could talk and sweat and cool away whatever troubles Clara thought they had back then — in the ways that he thought women must do. Sometimes they simply spent the day in that back yard of theirs.

And he would marvel at what Ellen could find in Clara — a brightness that was never there for him alone, never there, really, without her — although sometimes it would be a light inside

Clara for hours after Ellen had left. He could see that, no matter how distant from him Clara was. And so it came that he wanted to talk to Ellen about it — he wanted to know that part of her, too.

And so one day he called her.

That's how it all became Raymond's to carry, Raymond's for cause.

It still amazed him to realize that only two or three months after that call he came home to find a note on the dining room table, beside the ashtray full of broken cigarettes, lip-painted. The ashes flew when he lifted the square of paper.

Ray,

David is with Jeanne and Roger.

I'll call you in a day or two.

Clara

Simple enough that he could remember it all these years later. But then, what else had she needed to say?

On that day, the house had ticked as he touched the back of the chair she'd left he didn't know how long before. He had run his hand across it as he would her shoulders. To ease her. And then he realized that, while he wasn't surprised — how could he be? — he was afraid. He walked to the narrow kitchen and drank off three full glasses of water from the tap, looking out over the yard, thinking that the lawn needed mowing.

He had lifted that blue phone to call Ellen, of course, but instead he dialed Vic's number. He hadn't told his father every-thing, but only that Clara was gone.

"Thing's happen," the old man said, "Go get your boy, Raymond."

While his father spoke to him, Raymond had watched a raccoon walk slowly through the evening light at the back of the lot with what looked like a turtle in its mouth. Things like that happened from time to time, that part of town was cut by irrigation ditches and greenbelts. They lived with wild things that rummaged and tore through neighborhoods, things that howled and cried late at night.

"And when she comes home, Ray? —"

But he didn't remember ever seeing a turtle in Colorado before that. It must have been somebody's pet, slipped out and gone now like a lapdog in the foothills.

"Raymond?"

"You Dad."

"When she comes home? Don't ask too many questions."

Raymond had dragged his fingers through his hair just like Vic always did, and the motion had caught the eye of the animal in the yard. It stopped for a moment then and took Raymond's measure, his size and his distance. It undoubtedly judged him not to be a threat, one man inside a house yards away. And so the animal had turned a slow shoulder and slipped calmly into the evergreens. Raymond hung up the phone, then, and washed the glass, dried it with a fresh cup towel, put it away. He fetched his keys from the dining room table, pulled the front door to, and walked to the neighbors' — a few streets over — to retrieve his son.

For the next month, he took that David boy wherever he could, which he thought would be all right in that construction job he'd taken. The boy must have been about five years old then. They were building the new airport. Raymond had been in charge of the survey crews, and so he could take the boy along without much trouble. He thought it would be good to do that — and to make note of what the boy said and did. This seemed important to him then, this storing up. So Raymond took his son to the fields where they were marking new land for construction or excavation, the great squares of yellow line and painted pine stakes with concave tacks tapped into their flat tops, like the on-point tracks of little dancers. He was better at this job, Raymond was. Selling ads had never brought him anything but free time.

He showed David what the instrument was for, holding him up to the eyepiece, how to balance the rod plum, and even, eventually, how to throw the chain into its half-sized circle. To Raymond, the leather strops that secured the chains were suddenly like Vic's world had been, where what was held together was held with hides and a handshake.

There was more power and speed in the world now, he thought. And so, just to be safe, he'd have David sit in the Ford when the graders and land-movers were too close by. Only when it was nearest safe would he let the boy tag along, saying things to him like, "You stay close now, Davey" and "Step back there," things he had to say because of the world he worked in now. Things that made him regretful in the evening when he realized how little he'd let the boy talk, when that had been the plan all along, to hear him. Raymond had, at least, noticed David standing there beside him with his hip cocked and pocketing his hands the way Raymond knew he had always done. He was surprised that it had made him laugh into his hand with his back to the boy, made him wink to the chainmen and the operators.

But then, all of a sudden, it was too much of a burden, that imitation, too much to worry with when Raymond was working on something as basic as getting by without Clara. He didn't want to be making decisions that were bigger than he was. He didn't want to be anybody's guide — or their record keeper. But with his son's eyes on him that way, Raymond became a pattern anyway — a model at his worst moment, when he'd made mistakes he couldn't admit to, when all he could think was that Clara had left, that he knew why, and that he had nothing left to give his own son — not even good attention.

It took days before he could talk to Ellen that first time. He knew better than to call her the way he was. Of course, the phone rang in his house from time to time. He knew who it was and that she must have known Clara was gone — if for no other reason than that the phone went unanswered. But he couldn't imagine what they could say to each other — he and Ellen, what they even had a right to say.

On the slope of that mountain, Raymond rubbed his old mouth sideways with the palm of his right hand and then wiped the moisture from the loose corners of his lips. He squinted up at the whitening sky and thought he saw something fly a circle once in the thin air. Most likely it was a red-tailed . . . haw . . . hawk, floating the last currents of day. But Raymond couldn't quite make it out.

In the weeks before she left — every time — he would find Clara sitting at the dining room table in the evening, watching the smoke rise from between her knuckles. Most often she had slipped to an odd angle in the chair, her belly just rising against the cloth of her housedress. Her eyes unfocussed, her hair a great reaching lament. And she would answer Raymond's every question with a yes or a no and never lay the cigarette down.

"Your day all right?" he would ask her coming in with red airport mud on his rough-outs and the smell of smoke in his hair and his khakis.

"Yes," she'd say. "It was fine, quiet."

"Ellen call?"

"No, Ray."

And he wouldn't know what to say then.

"How was David's day?" he'd ask. Or something.

And then she'd say something like, "All right, I guess," all breathy as she punched out her cigarette. "He's around here somewhere. You could ask him."

"Well then," Raymond would answer her like he was about to begin something, because he was reaching with all his might toward the everyday. "I will."

And he would go off in search of his son. That was the way their conversations ran in those days, not that she had ever talked much from the start. What kind of fool was he to let himself believe that they could make it work? It must have been another world then — a world where women stayed. Or where fools expected them to — fools and infinite jesters.

High over his head, Raymond could hear a distant whining sound, and he lifted his eyes to the sky. A vapor trail insisted through the milling grey clouds. *God's speed* — a thought he always had since the war when travelers came to mind, what he said to the airmen on that carrier. It had started as a prayer for safety, their safety, but then it had become the understanding that things always happen all too fast.

Hre ↑ etch s pel

D. E. L. E. O. N., he thought, making the capitals in his head, spelling. Ensign, 38300775. Numbers. Pulled him off of General Parker's plane there at McClellan in 1942. Vic hadn't even known that's where he was. Everything he owned in that duffel. Almost nobody knowing he was there. Raymond looked around for that satchel. Everything. That little book Vic had copied out for him to carry, that ferns or phonog . . . or picture, really, of him and Clara at the tricksk, the . . .

"Trocadero," he said out loud without trying to.

Vic's first letters.

Somewhere in the Pacific that plane had gone down with that duffle and everybody. He'd thought it meant his life after that would lead to something important — that he'd been spared for some good goddamned reason. A thought that, returning here and now, made him bark at the mountain again. Then Raymond shook that old hand hard and long until it could move on its own, put it down on the paper, and wrote:

dfl fs slf nmnmn ys

She was gone that first time for over four weeks.

3

At the end of that long month, Clara was standing in the window when Raymond came home after work. He was at Fluorin then. That's right.

He had seen her there from the street and kept his eyes on the window as he pulled the company Ford slowly into the driveway. But he didn't get out. Instead, he sat still, listening to his car tick as it cooled and wondering whether he could or should go into the house with her there. The pink clouds across the window and the late day glare kept him from reading her face, but he could see that she was hugging herself like she did, and he thought she might have fixed up her hair. She was wearing a dress he'd never seen, and he was sorry to realize that it made his own arms heavy just to look at her.

He turned on the radio then, in part because it gave him a

reason to stay in the car, but also because he knew that almost any sound would help him to sort things out. Music had always done that for him. He needed to see ahead of time what he could ask her and what he just didn't need to know about. He wondered where David was. Out in the yard if she'd been brave enough to pick him up at school. Over at the neighbors' if not, waiting for his father to pick him up.

Raymond couldn't take his eyes off Clara, framed in the window like a reflection. He had expected her to be different, maybe spent or maybe reclaimed. One or the other. He didn't know — just different. But from where he sat she looked the same.

It had been a brisk fall day. The leaves on the cottonwoods and elms had turned but not yet begun to let loose. His favorite time of the year, when the geese from the parks began to fly from lake to lake as though they were going somewhere, though they'd be in the city all winter long. Much as he'd always been able to remember of that day, he never could recall the music that had been on the radio. But he knew that, finally, it hadn't helped him much. And eventually, because there was nothing else to do and because he knew that Clara could stand at that window all night long if he didn't come in, Raymond clicked off the radio, grabbed his lunchbox, and climbed out of the Galaxy. For some reason he had shut the car door as gently as he could. It seemed the right way to be, a way to control himself. Then he turned to look up the street. There was no sign of David there and he'd known that the boy must still have been at Jeanne's.

Raymond had shrugged his jacket straight and walked only to the walkway at the front of the house. He stopped before the window and looked at her through the dirty glass. He could measure her there. And she let him do that. It wasn't a new dress, but only a sweater he hadn't seen before, which she had pulled close about herself. As always, her waist was cinched tight — to keep in the heat of her, he thought — and her skirts flared at the hip in the way he liked. He'd been right about her hair: It was a little longer now and she'd wrestled it into pins so that her face was bared to him. He thought he could smell the lilac scent of her through the glass, and it made him shiver a bit. He had no idea what his face must have said to her. But he knew that she'd looked like the most complex goddamned woman he'd ever known. And all he really recognized in her expression was the sadness that had always aroused him, the way her mouth turned down just a bit, the constant moisture in her eyes.

When she blinked, slowly, he turned and stepped onto the porch. He'd hung a good, solid oak door on the front of that house, something real and substantial to represent the DeLeones to the world. It was the first thing he'd done to the house, a solid door with a brass knob that felt just like security in his hand. Vic had always said your front door is your stake — lets people know what you value. Raymond was proud of the way he had hung this one; the door that came with the house had been hollow and painted. This one showed its grain. He turned the knob to release it and then pushed the door quietly open with the palm of his hand. Its weight offered a pleasant resistance to him. And holding onto that knob was what gave him purchase to step into the house where Clara waited, like a package he'd have to sign for.

Raymond had stopped in the vestibule, noticed that David's little red backpack was not on the stairs. He set his briefcase and lunchbox down there, where his son's pack would have been, straightened himself soundlessly up, and then watched the slow motions of this strange familiar woman in his house. After a moment, Clara turned to face him.

He had nothing to say at first, though he had all the thoughts of what men were supposed to do at moments like that, what they were to say and do and the voice they were supposed to use. How they should stand. What righteousness is. And contrition. But he didn't know which was due. He knew he couldn't raise his hand, knew just as well that he didn't want to. It wasn't that.

When Clara didn't speak, he lifted his chin to signal that a minute or two would have to pass now before they could get anything said at all. He walked to kitchen and stood there a moment, feeling the electricity in his shoulders. He plucked the phone from the wall and marveled again that he'd let her buy an aqua-colored one. He slammed it back down hard enough that the bell inside rang a note from the force of it. When he'd gathered himself, he'd picked the set back up, dialed slowly, and counted the rings.

"Jeanne?" he'd said, his voice surprising him it was so tight. "It's Raymond."

She had begun to ask him something he didn't hear, but he had interrupted to tell her that David needed to stay the night with her son — whatever his name had been — if that was all right. When he'd made the arrangements, he hung that phone silently on its metal hook, picked it up again, replaced it, covered it with his hand, uncovered and covered it again — it was water and then flesh and then water again and flesh.

Raymond could see that now.

Then there was nothing for it but to go back to the living room.

Clara hadn't turned to the window while he'd been in the kitchen. She hadn't sat down either. She just stood there in the center of the room, perfectly still, with that face he couldn't read, waiting. When he stepped into the room, she had looked into him for a brief moment and then let her eyes fall to his chest, where they remained while she waited — and so he could study her again, more closely this time. She was letting him do that to her.

Her left arm hung at an angle along the front of her thigh; the other crossed her small belly and held the left at the elbow. She wore her ring. He had measured the length and thickness of her, the color of her skin, the hue of her hair. And in with everything he was feeling was the desire to whisper into her again, to lay his mouth into her hair and speak.

"Clara," he had simply said. It wasn't a greeting. Or a question. Or even a lament. It was just a naming, really, just saying her name because it was her name. But his voice made her flinch. Then she met his eyes again. And now, on this mountain, Raymond could hear her, way back away from him in that house of theirs:

"You and Ellen," she said, "you make me be . . . *still.*" Then she turned to the window. "If I didn't move, Ray, I wouldn't be able to breathe — like a shark, you know?"

That's actually what he remembered, the thought of her motionless in a cloud of blue water. The thought of his lost wife as another creature.

She had fumbled then for the pack of cigarettes in the pocket of her sweater. And Raymond recalled that the sound of the cellophane had seemed to comfort her. She had dug into the pack for a long time in a distracted way, with one ineffectual finger, as if only to make that sound.

He'd cursed then. He was sure of it. Made his hand into a weapon he wouldn't ever be able to use.

"I wasn't like that before, was I?" She looked at him but didn't really expect him to answer. "Anything I did would have been wrong, Ray. Whether I went up to make the beds, or picked up the phone to call you? Or if I went alone to the movies, applied for some job. Or broke up the garden, threw my coffee cup at the wall, let another man have me, Ray? Slit my wrists, cut off my hair, started dinner — it would all still be wrong. You know what I mean? And if everything is wrong, Ray, if every-thing you can possibly do is wrong? Then you might never do anything again. You just might — I don't know — freeze."

He wasn't sure of the exact words, but he remembered the rhythm of his own name repeating that way in whatever she said. Clara had laid the cigarettes on the windowsill then, with-out taking one out of the pack, and then she put her hands on her arms and turned her face away from him.

Raymond realized the door was still open and he turned his head to look over his front lawn. The light had turned golden and he could hear children. Without taking a step but leaning so that he was almost off balance, he reached out and, with just the tips of his fingers, sent the door to closing. For Clara. He always liked to let the dry, cool Colorado air into the house in every season, but he knew that she needed him to close them inside this house for now. And he knew that she would be chilled just then.

"So are you back?" he had asked her, his voice still tight.

Clara shook her head, once, violent and sorry. And her thick hair had broken free of the pins on one side. He had buried his hands in his pockets then and nodded, though she wouldn't see that. Raymond had already figured out that he would be all right without her, and so he knew he would be all right with however long she stayed.

And so, "All right," he said then. "We'll make do."

He walked into the room, turned on the lamp by the read-ing chair, and straightened back up with his mouth set. Clara had looked at him confused, and he had been pleased that he could read her face again.

The mountain wind cupped around him, colder still, and Raymond scooted back into the rocks as best he could. It ached low in his back to move that way now, and he wasn't sure that he could feel his legs. He leaned sharply forward, and then pushed himself toward his knees, farther than he thought he could still bend. He reached out into the cold and picked up his stain, his . . . his stick — no. . . his cane. Then he used it to croup everything within his reach. He saw that the pen was still in that other hand. It seemed he couldn't put it down. And now the walking stick was in the one.

But Raymond was thirsty and he wanted to open that wha— that, water baw . . . that . . . oddle. Trying to decide just how to do that with these things in his hands he thought about all this remembering. He wasn't sure that what he heard in his head was what had been said, because he knew that words were changing things now. There had probably been a lot more to that talking with Clara. Words weren't what he could call anymore, since all this trouble. He didn't even really know whether he'd played her voice in his head or only thought he had — thought he had remembered, but hadn't. It seemed that he only remembered by seeing — not hearing, really — and he didn't know why it all came to him in high colors and mists and fogs and waters. Before, when he thought about that long ago day it didn't have any color at all. It was more like the pictures on his dresden. Was that what you call it? He'd often wondered about that, about how, over the years, he'd washed all the color away somehow.

Now it was back.

Raymond hit the cane on the ground a couple of times until his hand let it loose. He opened the bottle with his teeth again and drank. Then he wondered where the cap had gotten to.

That's when that David boy began to climb — the day when he found his mother back home, though he was only six or seven.

At first it was only up onto the picnic table, or onto one of the redwood benches. And then, a little later, it was into the first fork of the cottonwood. Month by month, as his reach grew, he climbed higher. Whenever Raymond came in from work, the boy would be out in the yard somewhere, in one costume or another. He'd always done that. He'd be as high in the tree as he dared, no higher than Raymond's head at first. But up there alone, David would imagine worlds. He'd tell his father and then his grandfather about oceans and voyages, about old ships and handmade . . . rafts all wattled and stacked high with wood against the waves. It was as though just lifted onto that first wide branch of the cottonwood, his David boy wasn't any longer in their little dry-nested city.

He would talk of all that at night when Raymond would tuck him in. It was about the only thing Raymond could do right in those days, tuck some little boy into bed and listen to him for as long as it took. Usually, there had been nothing in the house to pull him away from that small voice, and it had pleased him to watch the boy story himself to sleep. So Raymond held on to that task even if Clara was home. It kept him from facing her in that kitchen where she always spent her hours whenever she came back to them.

"How far can you see?" Raymond would say, up the trunk of that old tree. Or some such thing. And there would always be a long silence then, as though the boy was bringing the distance into focus before he answered, wanting to get it right.

"I can see Pike's Peak over that way," he'd point south. "And all the way past the city out there," he'd swing his arm around to the east.

But the tree wasn't that tall and the boy wasn't that high in it.

"You see Mecca, maybe out there, too?" Raymond would ask then. "Or just Kansas?" It didn't matter what he said, really, so long as there was distance or surprise in it. That's all a boy needs at that age, just a house and a tree and a word or two that sounds like some other place. And that was all he could bring to his son anyway, unknowable names and words like "Letheward" and "slugabed" — there those dark butterflies were again.

"Naw sir," David might answer back, "Just the capitol. It's gold and all by itself up on a hill." Despite what his father might say to him, and his own imagination, David always knew what was real.

The boy knew, too, that inside that house over there was his mother who didn't believe in anything anymore — except maybe in what she was afraid of.

On every return, Clara would fall deeper into the routines she came to depend on in that house. She'd free herself from Raymond's closeness early enough in the mornings that she could get up and make the boy's lunch and have some breakfast on the table for all of them in good time. She took to cleaning, too, and she had a schedule for the meals: roast on Sundays, chicken on Mondays, tuna casserole Tuesdays, and so on to the burgers and carrot sticks on Saturday night. She did the laundry on Thursdays, and the shopping on Tuesday. Every other Friday they'd go out, leave David at Jeanne's.

Looking down at the book on his thin lap, Raymond saw that he'd made some kind of tick marks on those wide pages. He wondered if he should go ahead and write it down, that schedule of Clara's. Make a record, since there's no one else to.

After a few weeks, after he'd decided to, decided what mattered and what he couldn't ever find, they made love or tried to. And then they'd try again another night, until he'd get angry at the both of them.

Finally, then, they could. And it would be different somehow, lasting a long while, or that's how he remembered it now. By then, all their rhythms had reached steady. Theirs and David's.

And Ellen. And then, while he was still watching his wife close, she would begin to slow herself toward stillness again, like a ball running uphill.

"Oh," she'd say, surprised when he came in. She'd snuff out her cigarette then and prattle on. "I'm sorry, darling," she'd say. She had never called him darling before all that. "I didn't get anything together for supper. What day is it?"

"Clara." He remembered laying his hand on her like Vic had taught him to do and then trying to reassure her of something, anything. It didn't matter. How could he do that, day after day?

"I thought this was what you wanted for a while." And his hands would wave about like they could stir the air.

"Yes," she'd answer and he'd know she wanted to mean it, but that wouldn't matter either.

"It was."

And then she'd rise up without looking at him and head into that narrow, pink kitchen he'd bought for her — a place that was solid and easy where she might be sure.

Her wide skirt filling the door for a moment, her waist cinched tight enough to keep her upright, she'd turn the radio on in there, to the serious music, and pull out a skillet to griddle the meat on salted iron with pepper and what Vic had always called What's-this-here sauce. For just a moment, it would all look normal and everyday from where he stood. But then he'd hear her sounding out below her breath wordlessly, already forgetting he was there. It wasn't a tune she'd make, but just a hum, like some distant roaring oven.

It was the same like that, over and over as the years ran, so that he could hear her leaving in the hum of her voice, deep and ancient, hot and distant, feel all of it slowing down. And to pass by that thought, maybe to put it off a while, he'd walk into the kitchen and up behind her and lay his hand on her waist, pausing a moment to see what would happen. She might lean her head his way, and he'd know there were still a few days to have her.

But she might not give any sign he was there. And if that happened, he knew that she'd pack a bag some day soon when David was at school, write another note, phone to tell Ellen that she needed some more time, and then disappear. Ellen always told him not to ask — just like Vic had said. She said she understood the way Clara was. She said that Clara would be fine and would come back to them in a few weeks, and that maybe the next time Ellen would just take off with her.

He never understood how they were together, the three of them, and he chose to believe all that because whenever Ellen would phone or chirrup hello through the open front door, some switch would be thrown in his wife. Ellen *did* seem to make her happy, even then — so much so that Clara would play the sport, act like nothing mattered but Ellen herself. And whenever that happened, he would find the two of them standing hip to hip in his kitchen, smiling at him, like the day was just a lark and nothing in their lives together could be any better. Why wouldn't a fellow tell himself that something like honesty and light would hold them together? He wanted to believe that Clara was only angry with him — in some shapeless way — and that they would one day settle into some kind of happiness, at least the kind that Clara's old white melancholy used to cause in him.

Each time they failed, David would come into the kitchen in the morning and ask where she was. More often than not Raymond would answer just by lifting a couple of fingers, because after the first few times, he could see in the squint of his son's eyes that the boy understood — that Raymond didn't have to say a word. And the older David got, and the more times that morning came to pass, the less the boy let on that he gave a damn where she was. Or — eventually — Raymond either, really.

That was when Raymond started writing things down, when he'd finally lost David to the boy's own understanding. He made his notes like Vic had always done — though what Vic had put into his notebooks were mostly somebody else's words, lines of other men's poetry, the simplest sentences of philosophers and politicians and historians and even naturalists.

It was one of those soft old notebooks filled up with collective wisdom in Vic's handwriting that the old man had sent with Raymond into the Pacific war. Raymond had pulled that journal out and turned the pages from time to time. But he would stop reading whenever the words sounded familiar, whenever he was afraid they would start to look like orphans gathered together for some official reason. The notebooks smelled like Vic's tobacco, and maybe that had been enough.

It felt now like it was.

So Raymond started making his own record. He bought a stack of small brown books with sturdy covers at a stationer's on Curtis Street. It was surprising how few of them the years had filled up, but at least what was in them was his own — as much as it could be. He'd meant to mark the days of David's unmothered life in those books — the boy's notices and accomplishments. And he'd been pretty faithful, really, in marking down his son's merit badges and commendations, the day he'd passed out throwing fastballs when it was 99 degrees on the mound, how that curved scar on his knee had happened, and later how much his first car had cost and its mileage, the boy's grades. He'd left out all the girls' names, though, and a whole lot else he thought wasn't any of a father's business. But fairly early on, other notes started to find their way in there too. And though he knew it wasn't for the first time, it struck him now that David would probably be reading in those books pretty soon. He wondered what all his son would find in there.

He ought to write down that schedule of Clara's. Right here on the green lines.

"Matter," Raymond deLeone said into the collar of his great coat and either winked or flinched against the blow. Then he sucked on his teeth and lifted his chin a bit just to reaffirm some dignity. Become a wordless man talking to himself. But at least he was finally taking hold of something, taking on some plan what took some effort. Getting up here in the cold — by himself. He let go of the water bottle and pulled the pen from that hand. Then he laid it and the jor . . . the *journal* — down by his leg and buried his hands in his pockets.

"'Matter." He shook his head, or the cold did, or all this trouble.

The last time Clara left, there wasn't any note. Not from her. David was only about twelve years old then, so you'd think there would have been enough of his life to fill more notebooks, more than that one stack on the middle shelf.

After a few months, Raymond had finally told Vic that Clara was gone for good this time. He also told his father that even if she came back he wouldn't be letting her into the house. He didn't tell him the other part.

So Vic hadn't argued but only said that either Raymond and David should move in with him there in the valley or Raymond should bring the old man up to Denver to stay.

"David will need that, Ray. And me too one of these days. Maybe already."

But Raymond didn't have an idea what to do.

"We'll let you know, Vic."

He'd never had to make another decision about Clara, because they never heard from her again. And though he'd lived with the thought of her and put some of that down in those notebooks, and though David had become more quiet and distant, the boy never again asked him about her. Not once in all those years. Of course, from then on he never asked much of anything, really. Raymond took to going in early to work, before David had even left for school, and showing up at home when it was evening, always after dark. Then he or the boy would put together some kind of dinner and he'd struggle to make David talk about the day. But the boy wouldn't say much. By Junior High, David had already moved into his own corner of the house, behind that closed door and under all the music he had in there, until their never seeing one another in the daylight seemed to darken the house itself. Each morning, when Raymond would open the drapes across that front window, it seemed to have less effect on the walls and the furniture. It got to where he thought a fog had settled in the front room.

So that summer, he'd sent the boy off to a camp somewhere near Elbert, bought a new pick-up — a maroon Ford half-ton — and went to get Vic. Driving down the Valley Highway, with his face into the sun and the Front Range huge and shadowed on his right, with the windows open to the thin dry air, Raymond thought how quick it was that a family could move into silence. That's the real danger. Even a family as wordy as the deLeones. Over the smooth miles he wondered what had brought him to all this quiet until, somewhere north of Huerfano County, he saw that he could draw a straight line from his falling for Clara's sadness on Fifteenth Street to his having no one at all to talk to anymore but a few spineless notebooks.

He was hoping Vic could fix all that.

When Raymond arrived, Vic had been sitting on the porch with five or six cardboard boxes stacked by the door. Laid across them was his pillow. Vic was smoking in his chair and watching the sun set. When Raymond turned into the lot, his father rose up slowly with both hands, squinting against his cigarette or from the pain of getting up.

"Vic," Raymond had nodded, mounting the steps.

The old man had put that little hand on his son's shoulder, just as Raymond had wanted him to. But it didn't seem to weigh so much anymore. Raymond had wrapped his arm around his father's back.

"Good to see you, boy," Vic said. "House seems a bit airy lately."

"I see you're ready," Raymond had said, looking the boxes over. "But I thought we'd stay the night."

"Well, I'm all packed up," Vic said, not quite arguing, but almost. "We get up there to your place, we can settle in." He was quiet a moment, but Raymond knew not to answer. "Where's the boy?" the old man asked then, glancing at the pick-up.

"He's at camp this week, Vic. You got anything in the house to drink?"

"Got just enough," Vic nodded and went in to get a couple of glasses of something.

Raymond turned to the porch rail and looked around the

place. It was the circle of space around the house that had always interested him. The line of cottonwoods was turning to charcoal in the late daylight, and he could see the shadows of waterbirds coming in over the river, probably herons. Beyond that were the Sangres, rolling over like old men. The grass between here and there was burned brown by the summer. And the sky curved all of it in so that the valley was completely isolated and safe and steady. Somebody rumbled by in a Chevy pick-up and waved a long arm uncertainly out the window. Raymond waved back by reflex and thought again how distance comes near. The palette of the valley — from the royal blue sky, through the purple mountains, the olive grasses, the charcoal bosque — was a dark quilt to Raymond, something heavy that soaks heat and lays it back into a body whenever the dry breeze brings the kind of chill that makes a home.

With his nose and mouth burrowed into his great coat, Raymond let go a sigh that warmed his chest. He smiled at the sensation and had a sudden wonder at how grey the hairs were in that hollow place.

"This all you're bringing, Vic?" He had asked his father after that first drink. Raymond remembered now how light the boxes had been, all but the two that carried the old man's books.

"If I take more than this," Vic had said, "won't be nothing to come back for."

"How about you take the guitar? For David, anyway."

"He play?"

"Nope."

And Vic nodded. "All right then."

They drank their supper that evening. And they talked the hours away without saying anything that mattered much, or anything Raymond could recall — just marking the changes in the night sky and avoiding the subject of Clara or what had finally broke her, waiting for the time when the drink would close their eyes. When Vic had finally gone to bed, Raymond sat at the kitchen table and began to write in one of those brown notebooks he carried all the time by then. And, although he never did go back to read any of it, he could remember that on that night all of the pages he'd filled up had been about the way the house smelled and how it sounded. How much it seemed to be the sensible trace of Vic, the floors scored by his boots, the doorframe yellowed where he put his hand every morning to steady himself on the way outside, the kitchen stocked with only two or three pans and a couple of plates. The smell of coffee and chilis and smoke was part of the walls.

Raymond had speculated how it might have compared to the house Clara had grown up in. That lost place on the high plains. He didn't think she'd ever said one word about what she thought of the valley — or of Vic.

And he remembered that some of what he'd written was angry and some of it sorry and that all of it was carried on the vapors in his glass, which was almost always the case in those years, and reason enough for him never to read any of it.

But that had been the last time, really, that he'd let himself get to the bottom of a bottle so fast that it made a mark. At least until Vic died. It had seemed all right on that night, somehow, since his own son was safely distant and he wasn't going anywhere, and his father was alongside.

Whatever he'd put down, Raymond had written until his eyes burned and the hot skin on his neck was rubbed raw. He'd written all the way till dawn, when Vic came back into the kitchen and started the coffee boiling. Looking at the book and then at Raymond, Vic had smiled just a little, the way he did, and then asked him about it, pointing with his chin.

"So. You about done with that now?" he'd said.

Raymond hadn't been able to answer. He knew Vic's question hadn't been about the writing. And in that way they had become a family of men, which had never been the kind of life Raymond expected.

He had no idea whether Vic would take to Ellen. And by then, it mattered — things being what they were.

Shall we go downtown?

The next morning they'd set out driving back to Denver, and that night had settled Vic into the bedroom at the end of the hall. By the time Raymond brought David home, Vic had set himself to make a project of the boy. Or that's the way it seemed to Raymond. Vic's boxes all were unpacked by the end of the week. His books were on the shelves, his few clothes hung up straight or folded away. And the old man had a satchel that seemed to be waiting for something, lying there on the bedroom table. He'd spent a great deal of time in David's room those first days, just looking at the walls and fingering the stuff on the boy's desk. And when they'd driven up to the house, he and David, Vic had been standing at the window, waiting, just where Clara had stood. But, unlike her, the old man had come right out the door before David and Raymond had untangled themselves from the pick-up. He hadn't called anything out to them but came onto the little concrete porch, buried his hands in his hip pockets, and smiled slyly. When David approached the house, his knapsack over his shoulder and a blanket under his other arm, Vic's smile had gotten wider.

"Hey, Vic," the boy had managed, looking sideways at that thin old man.

Vic had taken the step he needed to close the gap between them and laid that hand on David's head, tussled his hair a little bit.

"There still trees in the woods out there, Davey?" Vic had asked.

David shook his head almost imperceptibly and muttered something back at this grandfather.

"Well, with everything like it is. You know," Vic had said, taking the knapsack off his grandson's back, "you never know."

Or some such. "You never know" had just been one of the things Vic always said.

Pretty soon Vic began to set up rhythms. "It's what you're supposed to do, Raymond, whenever somebody in the house starts to get confused."

When Raymond came home from work in those days, he would find his father sitting out in the back yard under the old cottonwood, usually smoking or about to, rolling a cigarette and sometimes talking, sometimes not. At first when he saw Vic speaking out loud into the evening air like that, Raymond thought that his father might have what Clara had suffered through. He'd thought there might be something in the house, or under that raggedy tree, that stilled folks while driving their minds to other places. But then he realized that every time Vic was out there like that, it was because David was up in that tree again. And it wasn't as though Vic worried about David falling — Raymond knew from his own boyhood endangerments that Vic didn't indulge in catastrophic thinking. It was just that the old man seemed to think he needed to be visible to the boy all the time.

And then Raymond realized that Vic was probably doing the same thing to him.

When he'd hear the creak of the back door, Vic would lift his eyes from his book, and push up off his thighs, squinting against the smoke. Then he'd say something just loud enough that his voice would carry to his son across the yard, though he was talking to his grandson up in the cottonwood.

"Middle man's here now, boy. You see far enough from up there to know what's for supper?"

And David would call down at them both with something of a smile in his voice, something Raymond never could call out of him.

"Looks like steak and mashed potatoes from up here, Vic."

From the back porch, Raymond couldn't see his son among the wide cottonwood leaves. But he could trace the path David's voice would take through the rough limbs and across the stone patio. And he could feel the pulse of Vic's words bouncing across to him in the shade, reverberating between the thick branches and the hard ground. And the regularity of all that pulsing began to seem like the rhythm of home to Raymond. A couple of times, after they'd eaten whatever Vic could stir up for supper, Raymond would bring out the guitar and push it on the old man, wanting to hear that passable voice again while he and David cleaned up the dishes. But Vic would just say that his hands didn't work any more.

Raymond remembered the face on David every time that happened. The boy would look like a shadow of some sort was passing over the place, even though it might be just a constriction of the eye. Maybe the boy thought there was something important in that guitar and in his father's urgings about it. If so, he knew it wasn't anything that had been passed on to him. That's the way the boy's face looked. Just like that.

"Every time really," this old Raymond said into the wind, and then he smiled that he'd had no trouble at all speaking that out loud. It felt good not to have to wait out the changelings sometimes. In fact, he didn't even know that could still happen. Most often now he had to weave his way through a field of exploding airy noises before letting his mouth open. Or he'd just embarrass himself. That's why Raymond had to keep the habit of quiet all the time now, even though there usually wasn't anyone around to hear him in that house. Oh, David still came by a couple of times a week and called just about every day to make sure Raymond could still get up and answer the phone. He was a regular boy, Raymond thought and then laughed a little, ran his fingers through his thin hair, knocking his cap off and then bumping his head against the rocks. Probably raise a lump. He bruised so easy now. And the colors took a long time fading. His hands were always purple and hot.

A regular boy's used to cost six bits, he remembered. Every Saturday morning at George's on Colfax. He hadn't thought of that old Kraut in years or weeks really. David took him out every month or so now to get a trim at that place in the mall. Villa whatever it was. But back then — when he was a regular boy — come summer, David would have George run the clipper all over his head. He called it a burr, George did. A brrr.

Raymond shivered on purpose, and then he chuckled.

"Brrrrrr," he said and tried to shrug himself a little warmth. No matter how long he kept himself still against the same place on the rock face, it never did warm up. He was beginning to feel the cold running through his back, deep inside, making its way toward his lungs. He had brought himself here. That was act enough. Wasn't it? The boy would see that.

David called his father every day, just about.

The wind blew high in the arms of the trees, and Raymond looked between the gap in the rocks, down the slope, and wondered about his grown son — who probably knew he was gone by now. David was all the time worried about this and that. Always had been. So he'd made the house safe for an old man having all this trouble. The storm, no, stirt . . . the . . . the stove, really, didn't work anymore. David had unhooked it from the gas for some reason. But there was a little, some kind of — kit with a fan inside it, whatever you call that, and a turning thing made out of glass it looked like. So Raymond could heat up a bite to eat without using the — st . . . stove. Or setting everything afire, he guessed. And all over the house, David had undoubtedly put these flat, white shields in the outlets that Raymond couldn't get out with that old hand, even though his nails were still strong. So he couldn't plug in his razor, or anything else. But there were three cordless ones that David kept charged up for him somehow. Raymond had always hated going to bed without shaving, his whiskers tearing at the pillow and all. Women hate it, too, he thought.

Shall we go downtown?

Raymond sighed and realized there was a rattle in his chest. When he cleared his throat, something alive rustled away from the rocks to his left and a little cascade of gravel and dirt ran down by his boots. He picked his stick up slowly and looked over his head, kept still and quiet for a time, until the colored shapes on the stones began to interest him again. They looked a little like animals, a little like faces, a little like the curves of women.

David had told him just to use the shower stall in the master bathroom. Didn't want him stepping in and out of the tub, he said. Which was all right with Raymond. The tub was for Clara.

So he'd been pretty safe, really, in that old house. And he didn't go out at all, except to the backyard where everyone of them had been at one time or another. Raymond figured that right now he was out about as far as he'd been in years, up here in the stones. Out, steady in the wind, silver light, wave, wing when he ought to be home, he thought. Clara would be wondering where he was, or Ellen would, and he was sorry for that, though he didn't think he could get up to go just now. Maybe when it warmed up a bit.

Raymond slipped his hand into the chest of his great coat to warm it. And he felt something crinkle in the pocket of his shirt. He dug around in there for a good long while, trying to make that cold hand cooperate. But he couldn't get the first finger to work against his thumb with the paper in between them, down in there against his chest where he couldn't see to will them closed. In the grey white hairs of it.

It's a patient thing he thought, knowing to keep at it until that hand did what he wanted, almost by accident — patience he'd had to learn, really, since he'd had all this trouble. It wasn't natural to him, but if he stayed at a thing long enough it usually got the job done, and he was reconciled to that because it made him maybe more like his father.

Vic never had been hurried. And after he came to live with them, that seemed to make a difference to the way the boy felt about things. Though maybe Raymond hadn't seen it then, David started moving a bit slower and less in a straight line. And he started talking again — not about real things, of course, just matter-of-fact talk, with Vic, mostly. The boy was still all the time up some tree or other, but when he was on the ground his face wasn't all flushed up like he was angry anymore. More often than not, Vic would take his long legs over to meet his grandson coming out of the school in the afternoon, and Raymond had wondered what they talked about on those slow walks home. Probably this or that about Raymond having to be at work all the time now and how important it was for a fellow to have a job to do, how having chores helped you to give a damn.

That's what Vic had always said — that when a fellow does the work of hands, he comes to see that working matters and that life is at least a little bit of progress. Not a hell of a lot for most men, he'd say, but a little bit. "You need a hammer or a shovel or a pocketknife, Raymond. There ought always to be a tool in your reach. It scares off the apathy."

Raymond was satisfied with that and pulled his hand from

inside his coat. He checked to see if the paper was in his fingers. It wasn't. Then he troubled the pen back up from the ground since they were warmed up a bit. He opened the journal flat on his lap and set to writing again, remembering that he wanted to make some kind of record:

Iv scaaa rt of thphy

Raymond stared for a long while at the marks he'd made. He could see that they looked a little like words, but he could also tell by the pink lines that the letters weren't straight. He thought they seemed spaced oddly, too. Maybe he should turn the sheets a little bit next time and concentrate harder. Then he began to doubt that anyone would be able to read marks like these at all. Not that it mattered really.

"Matter."

Writing was something the other side of habit for him anymore, so he'd just have to keep trying — if that hand would stay warm enough. And it usually was. Vic had always said you should save reading and writing for after dark, but by the time the soul went down today, Raymond figured it would be pretty late in his life.

He set the pen into the crease at the center of the open book, cupped his hands together to make a hollow place, and blew warm into the emptiness he'd made. Then he bounced his legs a little to get the blood up.

In the late light, the silver patterns on the pen sang blue

in the wind and he blew in his hands. Raymond chuckled at that. It'd be good if those words worth sensible. That's what had begun to trouble him, really, and what had brought him out here — the sudden wonder that all his memories were just half-seen things and that words had become accidents he suffered.

"That reminds me very little of the time I took your daddy to see what they told us was The Last Buffalo." He heard Vic talking to him from somewhere. No, not to him; Vic was talking to David, making that same old joke about being reminded very little. He could just hear Vic telling somebody one more time about that used-up animal at the Fair with the fur falling off his shoulders like off of that old woman's, the one he'd given Clara's orange to. Raymond had asked him that day what would be left when the buffalo died. He'd believed somehow that the last one to go would have to leave a trace. He didn't mean a hollow in the air or ash on the ground or the smell of carbon, like from the street lamps in town. He had thought it would be something permanent. Not because the animal was dead; as a boy of five on a non-working ranch, Raymond knew about animals dying, and a little bit about losing people.

"After all," he said to the mountain.

His mother had died birthing him. But this thing, this last buffalo, had seemed different to Raymond, because the dead Last Buffalo would mean that a whole shape in the world would be gone. As though something real had become made-up. Vic always said the end of that conversation had come up quickly when Raymond asked one of those questions they said he always asked: "Are angels and giants not real because they all died?" When Vic had needed some clarifying of a question like that, Raymond had always tried again. "When that one's dead, are buffaloes stories?"

Vic's laugh was always in his eyes and not very often in his mouth. But maybe he could remember that only because Vic had taught David to do the same thing — to hold on to his amusement like a secret. Vic didn't ever laugh or sing, or pick up that guitar, in the years he lived in Raymond's house. But he had talked, all the time, especially to his grandson. He had talked to David through all the boy's in-between years when Raymond couldn't. That was back when the only thing Raymond could do was work the day away and then wonder through the night why he had done such a thing to drive Clara away from him like that. Wonder sometimes what David must be thinking, quiet as he was, so often configuring to be outside whenever Raymond was at home.

But all those voices and generations of men were collapsed now. They weren't much more than light, really, floating memories glowing cold above Raymond's head like whatever you call it, memories he couldn't write about or even call out loud anymore. Maybe all that time not talking — just listening to Vic and David and old Lacey down at Fluorin, listening to his own longing for Clara — maybe all that silence, is what had made him lose his voice. He knew that his quiet way was what made David all edges around him now. And now there was no changing it. There were hardly any words at all anymore. Oh, his son called and came by pretty regular, but he seemed almost angry whenever he had to fix the house back up because Raymond had spilled his dinner or lost his glasses or left the water running. And David got frustrated when Raymond couldn't quite say what he was talking about. Sometimes it was as though he thought it was Raymond's own fault that the words were lost.

And maybe it was.

Raymond cleared his throat again and wiped his mouth with the back of his hand. Then it struck him of a sudden that maybe God took a fellow's words away on purpose. Maybe He made those dark butterflies out of them so that whatever an old man was supposed to discover in his mind would stay secret, between him and God. Secret so that David and everybody else would still have to find it out for themselves. Whatever it was. Maybe that's why old men look confused from the outside. Maybe old is just not telling.

dfl fs slf nmnmn ys

"In many ways," Raymond said, and then he began trying to think about what might be hiding in all the changeling words that he hadn't known before. Sometimes over these past years or weeks, really, lights showed up in odd places just to attract his attention. And when he got closer to them they changed colors. There were voices in the air from time to time, too, and some of them weren't familiar. He knew that he felt better with animals around him, especially wild ones. But mostly he knew about being quiet. Words never said the whole of what you meant anyway. Clara's never had. Or David's. He wasn't sure about Vic. Sometimes, he thought, words can open up quickly — like sudden ... shoots, like ... tubes that can move you toward something good. But usually you never get there.

The only thing Raymond was sure he'd learned late was that you should look up at the circle, the — what was he trying to say? — the render, damn, the *horizon* from time to time. In fact, he knew you should move around at least enough to change where the circle is so you can tell there's more to being than what is inside it. And undoubtedly the higher you climb the farther you can see.

But then it seemed like David had always known that, and he wasn't old. Not like Raymond was. And not like Vic had been.

4

"It's too dark to feel in here."

That was Vic's voice in his ear again, and Raymond raised his eyes to the darkening sky. If he remembered right — but then, he knew that hadn't been a sure thing for a long while — Vic had turned on a lamp in every room he ever entered.

"Damn the darkness," he'd joke.

In those few years with him and David in Denver, the lamplight had glowed a flat line beneath Vic's door, no matter what time of the night it was. Sometimes Raymond would slip down the hallway to check on him, or just to listen, and from time to time, he could hear Vic mumbling in there alone, like he was committing something to memory. He probably was. Even beneath his breath, Vic's voice had a rhythm that soothed, so that after a while it would seem that he was saying the same ten or twenty or thirty lines over and over. Every so often the words would break through from that whisper into Vic's smoky voice, and that would mark a beginning. Or a beginning again. Then Raymond would take himself silently back to bed, coaxing sleep by holding on to the sound of his father and the sense of order that came with it.

You'd think all those late night studies would have kept the old man's mind quick. But it didn't.

"In many ways," he quoted his father quoting somebody else. And just saying that out loud lifted Raymond out of the shallow sadness that had crept into his chest with the cold. He shifted his legs again and then drew them up and tucked the satchel beneath his knees, tried to wrap his great coat around his feet. Then he tried to think in a way that really connected, wondering if that was the same old satchel that Vic had always kept on the table in the back bedroom. He rubbed the leather in that hand, and then brought his fingers to his nose, wanting a bit of the Prince Albert smell. But that was too long ago.

The thought of that smell was good for some reason. And he decided he wanted to make a note of it. But he couldn't find the pen just then in the twilight, and he thought he heard wings over his head, which distracted him from what it was he wanted to do. For what was probably a long while, he searched the deep purple air, but didn't see anything moving.

Undoubtedly, David rose up from those first years through a youth that Raymond had thought of as dignified if not distinguished. The boy had never accomplished much, really, and he didn't seem to belong to any school clubs or whatever they're called. But he wasn't too much trouble either. There had been a few girls in the boy's life. Not that he'd ever brought them around, but he was out late most nights. Whenever he came in, he'd fix himself something in the kitchen and eat it there or take it to bed with him. But he never did stop at Raymond's room or at Vic's, even when all the men's lights were on. At night, the deLeones just didn't seem to cross paths. Maybe that was what you'd expect where he and David were concerned. But Raymond always wondered that Vic needed to be alone so often when the night tried to fill up the house. He was so much around during the boy's days. But at night he took to himself.

That was even more the case when David began leaving before dinner. With the boy out in the city somewhere, Raymond and his father were surprised to find themselves eating alone again. And the surprise had led them into a silence fed by Raymond's sadness, he guessed, but also by something in Vic that hadn't been there before — something that began just about that time as a shadow in his eyes.

That's where it started.

After dinner, Raymond would clear the table while Vic smoked. Then, as was their custom, Vic would step to the sink and begin his own slow process of doing the dishes, while Raymond pretended to read the evening paper at the cleared kitchen table.

Every now and then, Vic would hum this or that with the running water, but he didn't say a word to Raymond while he worked. Fact is, he never had spoken much when his hands were busy, not that Raymond could ever remember. What he learned about the right way to do things had come mostly through the laying on of his father's hands. To Vic, chores always seemed to be a door to something quiet and self-sufficient. Vic was alone and almost wordless when he worked, no matter what he was doing or who was around him.

So after dinner they both would just listen to the splash and rush of the water and to the real, everyday clacks of plates and pans. Sometimes, Raymond would glance up from his paper and be surprised again that an old man was standing there, doing the dishes, where Clara should have been. But whenever that happened, he'd gather up his voice and compliment the dinner out loud. Vic would wait a bit while he brought himself back into the room and then he'd nod and say, "Oughta sleep good tonight, I guess."

Then, whenever he'd let the water out of the sink, Vic would turn his back to the counter and dry his hands on one of Clara's blue checked towels, staring over Raymond's head out the back window. And Raymond would wonder at the blankness that seemed to be spreading from his father's eyes and beginning to dull the old man's face. Every night, Vic seemed to stare a little longer through that window, rubbing his hands in the thin, damp cloth without thinking about it. Finally, when something in his mind had been fully calculated or lost, he'd toss the towel onto the counter and say, "Welp," with a bit of a smack, "I wonder what's for breakfast." Always the same sentence. Then he'd turn away from his son like a bear changing its mind and head down the hallway to the books in his room — still pretty early — sometimes calling out a good night, sometimes not.

Late one evening Raymond went to take the garbage out, probably worrying like he always did whether David had gotten himself supper somewhere and where he might have gone to afterward. He just remembered being alone in the kitchen. Shaking the bag loose from the can, he heard a clank that was a bit too sweet for tin.

Vic had thrown all the night's flatware into the sack with the table scraps. After thinking on that for a moment, Raymond stepped over to the drawer just to check. Most of the knives and forks and spoons were missing from the 12-set Clara had bought when they got married — envisioning dinner parties or lots of children, he couldn't remember which. He matched that up with the emptiness in Vic, and then he realized that something really was changing. The old man had started searching for the names of things a little more often. He'd heard that some people begin to lose words and good focus when they age, though Vic was the first old man he'd ever known. And he wouldn't have expected such a thing of that old reader.

Between the high rocks, where his toes had begun to ache in those boots, Raymond shrugged inside his great coat and surveyed the darkening sky before him. His eyes eventually allowed a strong yellow glow above a ridge almost straight in front of him. At first he thought it was dawn coming on already, but he didn't think there'd been anything like enough time yet. Not that he could tell such things anymore, really. Seemed like every hour or so it was time for the next meal, or time for bed, or time for something else that was just a bother. Sometimes David would call on the phone even when it seemed like he'd just then walked out the door to his car. And just like Vic, Raymond could lose a full day at that kitchen window — especially if it was snowing. He'd always loved to watch the snow — the way it changed the lay of the land and made possibility into a good thing again. Raymond guessed he didn't know anything about time anymore. He wasn't even sure how old David was — thirty something he thought or maybe in his fifties.

But even if he couldn't gauge how long anything lasted these days, Raymond still knew that if Clara was alive somewhere, she was almost as old as he was — both of them older than most of the naked little trees there on that mountain. The truth was that he thought about age and years whenever he remembered she was gone — for months and days and years. And it seemed as though that always happened to him at the same time. It was always right after his breath had caught on the realization that he couldn't find her in the house — and then on how long it had been since he'd had the least idea where she was. He'd always said that Clara was *ineffable*. Now *that* was a word to call, and it made him smile at himself, though for the life of him he had no idea what it meant. Did that mean *gone*? That didn't seem quite right.

He wished he could pull those legs the rest of the way and tuck them under somehow where they might be warmer. But it hurt him to move them at all anymore. So he just shrugged himself up and tried to connect his mind back into the colors of all that remembering.

The dullness set up fast in Vic once neither one of them had the boy to talk to anymore. And with just the two of them in the house, it seemed like Raymond had begun to worry more about Vic than David. He was sorry for that. But young men are always all right.

Vic seemed to wander so that Raymond started to think he might lose the old man. Let him misplace himself. And so Raymond started to take days off from work, too many days, really — enough that he lost the job he had, whatever it was. That Fluorin job, probably, he thought — though it was a long time ago. He remembered being afraid the old man might walk right out the front door or cut himself with something or burn Clara's house down. He remembered thinking there wasn't anything else to do but stay home with him — and since they'd sold the place in the valley by then for good money, it turned out he could.

Vic began to search harder for names, stuttering and

pumping his head, trying any way to pull them off his tongue. Of course he was willful about it, like he always was about everything, keeping at it until even if he found the word the sentence would already be gone. It wasn't just the names of people that got stuck there in his mouth. He couldn't call what he held in his hand either, or what he needed Raymond to bring to him. Everyday names. And a night's sleep didn't help. It would start up like that first thing in the morning.

Eventually, Vic's fragments didn't quite fit together, and he began to stand still every now and then, as though he was trying to triangulate. Nearer the end, he started hearing things. One afternoon, when Raymond was checking the oil in the truck, Vic stepped into the garage.

"You call me?" he had asked.

"No, Vic. You all right?"

Vic had nodded unsurely and looked around the garage and out the open bay door, not searching for anything in particular, it seemed, but as though he just needed to locate himself inside it. And then he said, "Guess I'll keep fighting them in there," and jerked his head backward, toward the house.

It was a sentence that sounded good at first, almost funny, but Raymond was almost certain Vic hadn't meant to say "fighting." How can you tell such things?

"Who you fighting, Vic?" he'd asked anyway, just to keep the flow going for his father — as you'd do for a child so that he could feel himself connected by your good attention.

And then the old man's searching turned inward to the dense, hardened webs of his mind, the stiffening net that was bringing him to a halt.

"I don't know," he said at last, but not directly to Raymond. Then he slipped back into the house so slowly that the door clicked shut. And Raymond had forgotten what he'd been doing before his father came in.

Sometimes it was as if all the wind of his life had stopped full, and the air around him had grown too thick to breathe easy.

They struggled on like that for months, Raymond trying hard to make every moment seem normal and Vic calling out strings of words that added up to nothing. Sometimes they did sound right. And sometimes Vic seemed certain they were. He'd raise one eyebrow at his son and turn his head a bit away to point one eye at him, challenging Raymond for a response. Asking his son to let him know that he'd done it, that by dint of his will he'd been cogent one more time. And whenever that happened, Raymond would hope it was he who'd lost focus, hope that he was just being a bad listener. Maybe Vic was making a sense that Raymond — sad and selfish as he was — just hadn't kept up with.

Then he'd ask his father to say it again so that he could understand. But the old man's eyes would slide to the left for a second, disappointed to the center of his heart. He'd say some syllables then that weren't quite words but that sounded like apologies, and he'd let the conversation go.

Raymond would start talking then, about whatever came

into his mind. And he would keep talking for long minutes — because he thought that just might keep his father from becoming afraid.

And what would he do if Vic were frightened?

Then one night, when Raymond went to check on his father, he found Vic in that old musty platform rocker with a book open on his lap. Vic was staring at the yellowed pages, squinting hard like he did at one of his chores, shaking his head just enough that Raymond could see the surrender in it. Vic hadn't looked up when his son opened the door or when he entered the room. And he didn't answer when Raymond quietly called his name.

And that was the end of it really. Raymond talked on for another few weeks, but Vic would only quote a piece of this or that, something broken and smoky that he'd put into his mind years before. Like that king of infinite space —

For a while, Vic could still walk around safely and pour himself a cup of coffee, but that was about it. Then he began to wander the house, back and forth, looking for something or somebody he couldn't name. Raymond had to help him get dressed and be sure he had on two socks. He had to button the old man's shirt and even fasten up his jeans. Raymond would roll a cigarette for him every morning and set him at that kitchen table, watching to be sure the old man didn't burn himself.

Raymond liked to think that he took those long days finally to work everything through. He talked more into the room at the old man than he'd said since Clara had gone, or maybe even since the war. It could be that he was just trying to hold on to words since Vic had lost them all. But even through all that talking of this and that, mostly nothing, with his father in the room, it seemed to come on quick that Ray the Lion was alone. Vic looked as though he was listening, because he couldn't do anything else. But he was already gone.

And that was in those long years when David didn't need his father anymore and figured his father didn't need him.

And so one night Raymond just started in telling his life to an old man who might have understood and might not have, but who couldn't do or say a thing to help him get a handle on it.

"You know she started out sad, Vic," Raymond had said.

It wasn't anything that he'd done to her life, was it? It was like a white melancholy — that's what he'd always called it — something that glowed out of her, the kind of sadness that Raymond figured would make her dear and close and affection-ate. That's what had brought him to her, the kind of sadness that came with a promise, the sadness that rose up out of the most beautiful mystery he'd ever run into. Had Vic seen that in her, too? The way her hair haloed her and how whenever she was thinking or trying to decide about something her arm would cock to hold one hand upright — as though vertical was the most restful position. Her hand would balance itself on her wrist in a way that he thought the exact image of her life, or at least of how he first saw her life. So frail and fey, something tentative even in how she stood. How could a man not be drawn to that, Vic?

Were these real words? To Raymond now they were only melody, or something more real than that, something like breath.

They'd driven up to Los Angeles that one weekend, the only leave he'd had before shipping out. And through the entire trip, she had always seemed balanced like her own hand — but on the edge of a chair or the spike of her heels. She leaned against walls and railings whenever they stopped walking, usually against him. He didn't think there'd been a moment that weekend when she hadn't rested a hand on him as though to keep from tipping away.

And that Saturday afternoon they had taken a tour bus to the homes of the stars. She'd worn a wide hat against the sun and kept pressing it against her hair. But she insisted on riding on the top in the thick open air. And she had worn a flowered dress, he remembered. Across her shoulders, for some reason he didn't understand in the heat of the day, she had wrapped a thin blue sweater that gathered at her throat. And each time the bus slowed before some grand mansion between the palms, the shadow would lift from her face. Her green eyes would widen just a bit, and sometimes that spot between them would redden at some thought of what he did not know. So he asked what she was thinking and she said that she could tell from the great mansions that people are real.

He'd laughed at her then. She could make a man wonder.

— Don't you laugh at me, she'd said and pushed against him with her shoulder. You can see that they're real enough to walk through open doors and touch stones and gaze through windows. See that man there?

And she said that the cars in the driveways and the doors and windows, too, proved that rich and famous, starry people were just like us in some ways — if only by having to live with the same scale that we do, no matter how large their homes or wide their yards.

— That's just something you have to feel from time to time, she told him. You have to know that when you close your eyes or turn away home, or when you shut your door or fall asleep, the other people in the world are still real. And separate from you, you know what I mean?

That's what she said that day, Vic. That people don't simply disappear because you can't see or hear or touch them anymore.

And when we got off that bus, we went to a little restaurant on Vine Street and she just kept talking about it. It was as if she'd slipped into her own dreams in front of the houses of those movie stars. That was something in her that she had never talked about before. She was new again, Vic. And her voice was fresh and light, and the war was a long way away — for a few days.

She said it was the cities that made you think about everyone else, because there are so many other people there. They're at every corner and in the cars you pass going the other way, she said. And they're in stores that you've never even gone into before. And you just feel like they couldn't all be real without your looking at them.

Could they be? she had asked him. Could they be real without us?

— You, Clara, he'd said not sure that he could laugh about a woman who thought that way.

— Most of the time, she said then, you really don't think so, do you? No matter what you say about it out loud.

And so for one moment on a day like that one, he guessed, a woman like his Clara could see things differently.

She said that in the country, where she grew up — where the fields were almost endless and you went for days without talking to anyone outside your family — in large open places like that, she said, people aren't such an issue. Even alone in an open field, you know that you're real, she told him. And then she laid her hand high inside his thigh.

Had he really said that to Vic? It embarrassed him a bit even now to admit that Clara could think that way.

"You can smell the real in a place like that, Ray, even if the wind is blowing."

He could hear her sweet voice now. "So long as you're not thinking about other people."

But he'd just finally decided to laugh at her — laughed right out loud listening to her in that little restaurant they'd ended up in after that bus ride. And he remembered that his laugh had made her blush. Then he had asked her, so awfully asked her in the way that men always spoke to women in those days, as though they were only foolish and not full of knowing, the way women are, aren't they, Vic? He'd asked,

"Who would ever think other people aren't real, Clara?"

And she had answered him, with her face so colored by her rising blood that he could almost feel the heat of her from across the table.

"People like me, Ray."

And he had loved her even more for that — because she thought hard about what no one else seemed to consider at all. He loved her, too, because *he* believed right then that there just couldn't *be* any other people like her.

But Clara thought there could be. Even though most times she also thought she might be completely alone when she closed her eyes and that there could be other folks just like her — if she could only see them. In her sadness and her worry was promise, he thought. Clara was somehow attached by her trouble to something that he couldn't even imagine being true. And wasn't that hopeful? That she could believe what was out of the reach of all his thinking? He thought it was, and so it had become something like religion to him — Clara's everyday faith in the power her seeing had to create the world.

And then he had broken it.

Did he say that, too?

Some creature called out to the night. It must have been close by because the sounds weren't carrying anymore. Raymond knew this without thinking it.

What would you think, Vic, of such a thing alone in a perfect city under clear skies and filled with movie stars and dreams, riding in the open air beside a wife that beautiful and set in the earth who had picked you out of all the men around her? And then sitting beside her, proud to be there, in a fine little restaurant, where she was speaking her dreams out loud?

"What would you think, Vic?" Raymond now asked the dark and the steep slope of the cold mountain, just as he remembered asking his already lost father in that warm kitchen all those years ago. Vic listening about like the mountain was, he laughed.

Raymond knew that it probably didn't make any sense. But it was true that this was the way he had seen her sadness and her worry, right from the start. To him, her troubles were like a spring — the hope that what life was couldn't be what was intended. Surely there was more to come. And it had seemed to Raymond that Clara's worrying was the road it would come by. He knew she hadn't seen her own troubling time that way. But he had.

Raymond had.

Their son was conceived on that weekend, in that warm and starry place — in the privacy of a hotel of cabins with red tile roofs. Those solitary rooms, he remembered, combined into a stream that meandered through gardens and beneath a canopy of trees, somewhere along a twisting road that made you forget the city altogether. Clara's hunger through those two nights was as full as he ever knew it to be. A man wouldn't forget that, even all these years later when his words had fluttered away from him.

He had gone off to that pacific war six days later, working hard to believe like Clara did, that he could create the world just by seeing it. Vic could understand that, couldn't he? That going to war with such a faith is better than any charm could be. It was never the goal of any man soldier he'd known to win the war. Winning the war was somebody else's look out — somebody larger than they all were. The sailor's goal, the warrior's, always is just to get home again. You set that hope against the sickness in your belly during those long days at sea. You sleep with it wherever the Navy sets you down. You curl around it in the holes they make you dig in the sand. You will every bullet to skirt you with that one hope. It was what kept you from giving in to the heat and the bugs and the chatter you could hear through the jungle just before every dawn. And you listened to its soft voice when someone else's blood was on you.

Before then he'd never told Vic that he hadn't always been on a ship, that he wasn't just a sailor. Not a soldier, either. Something in between that they said he could never talk about, not even after the war.

It is damned simple to learn that you are fragile — especially in a war. But it's hard to see hopelessness. Which was merciful. Clara's seeing had taught him this. The hopelessness of someone else isn't ever your own. It never looks like that, and you don't expect it to. If you're alive and your eyes are open, even to see the dead is to wake up the hope that you'll make it home. Because you came this far already.

Did Vic know what he meant?

Seeing whatever you see, you make it true. Undoubtedly, Clara always understood that, or at least she had by the time she stepped off that bus in Hollywood. But he believed she'd known it before he'd first seen her — before he'd been made real by doing so.

Raymond pulled his shoulders to his ears and tucked his chin. He breathed warm into his coat. He could tell by the ache in his knees that the weather was changing. And he thought that he, or the fellow who wrote the note, must have bet on that.

It was night now and that would probably be enough to get this done. He looked up when he thought he heard a woman sigh. But there was nothing but the dark and the rocks and the shadowed arms of trees. And then the sigh again. He cocked his head to hear it.

Something had happened to Clara by the time Raymond came home. She was darker and had so lost faith that she could hardly speak. Maybe it was just because she had come to think that

Raymond was no longer true — because, gone to war, he was invisible to her.

But then, that made him sound more important than he'd probably ever been to her.

No matter how he worked to bring her back to him, he couldn't raise the blush on her again. Not so high as it had been before, and never again like that weekend in Los Angeles, when the war was only the lights off the coast and nothing was certain except what was in that red-topped cabin.

The doctors said it was the birth of the boy that made her so quiet — and not Raymond's coming home. But it never went away like they said it would. From time to time he had loaded Clara and the boy and piles of wool blankets into that old Buick and strained their way into the mountains for those high, thin summer picnics beside some rolling stream or other. You could still do that in those days and not run into people at every turn in the woods.

Clara would wear bright dresses and try her best, sometimes matching her small laugh to the sound of the water. He would try, too — splashing the boy's face or dipping his little feet into the stream. The cold water would make David scream and laugh and curl into a ball in Raymond's arms. Once, he took them up to Idaho Springs to pan for gold, and that was like the past and future all at once. There was still a little vial of the shining flakes they'd sifted out somewhere in that house.

It used to sit on the kitchen windowsill. Maybe it still did.

And Raymond started buying flowers and taking her out

to dinner whenever they could find a sitter. Doing all that he was supposed to do to make the time last.

But it never made a difference to her — that's how it happened, Vic — all the love Raymond had for her never seemed to make a difference. And when it happened, Ellen had taught him that you can't ever take ownership over anyone. You just borrow a woman's heart from time to time, Vic. Where she's been doesn't matter nearly as much as being able to see her every day — even for just a few months — to see her and imagine the way it once had been.

He always found hope in the scent of possibility that rose from Clara.

That's why, Vic, but it just didn't take, you know?

And so they tried again and again. Whenever she came back, he swallowed what burned in his throat, breathed as shallowly as he could, and took her in. For a few weeks after the difficult days of apology and searching — Clara would always give herself completely to them both, to him and the boy. Seemed like she would cook constantly, baking something for them almost every day. And she took new interest in whatever David was doing just then — his school and his playing, such as it ever was, the books he was reading, his friends, if he had any just then. At least for those brief weeks she looked for what might make her son happy and even threw little parties for him, though almost nobody ever came.

But for all her trying with the boy, David began to keep himself at arm's length from her. He grew into a kind of silence that hadn't been on him before the first time his mother left. Of course, he was still pretty little then, but that's when he started going out into the back yard and climbing up on that table, like trying to get up to their level, which didn't seem very high to Raymond. And then it was that cottonwood, Raymond laughed. If David ever learned anything up that tree, he'd never told his father.

After he was about eight or so, the boy wouldn't have much to do with her no matter what she tried. Of course by then she didn't know how to talk to him anymore, and Raymond sure couldn't help with that. David wouldn't go with his father anywhere either, not to work, not to a ballgame, not even on the errands. By then, David didn't say much to either of them. He wouldn't even help with the chores. But all that was before Vic had moved in, which had been a blessing

Looking back, it was clear to Raymond that each time Clara came home, he lost more of his son. It wasn't later that started. It was right then, the first time he found her looking out that front window.

It started when Raymond failed to react.

Of course, he'd been trained not to.

It must have been clear to David that the uncertainty of his life was as much Raymond's fault as Clara's.

That's how you lose a son, Vic — by causing his uncertainty. Or by his believing you did. If you make him sure about you and send him away, he'll come back, stay in touch, include you. That's us, Vic. But if he leaves home uncertain of you, he always will be. And he won't ever call where you are home again.

"I guess we didn't have much ground that was sure when the boy needed us to," Raymond had told his lost father there in that hot kitchen. Vic had raised his head, then, and quickly turned it Raymond's way, as if he could still be surprised. Then he seemed to nod, but it was so slight that Raymond couldn't tell what the old man meant. And then, Vic looked at his son as though he was trying to figure out who this fellow was and what exactly he was talking about.

In the dimming light, a short-tailed animal with yellow eyes appeared before Raymond — frozen in the gap of the rocks at his feet. It looked big enough that he imagined he could hear it breathe, trying to identify the sour smell of an old man. But the creature wasn't so large that Raymond was afraid. For what seemed like minutes, they both were perfectly still — for as long as Raymond's cold joints would let him be. When the pain of stillness was more than he could take any longer, he waved that cane at the yellow eyes and the soft dark shape around them. And then they were gone.

"What sow — souch sss ROUGH . . . *Beth. . .* ?" the change-lings flew loud from Raymond because he let them. He knew he sounded wild making such noises as all that. And so he bran-dished that stick just for the old fun of it, laughing at himself for speaking tongues to God's animals. But the laughter fell off of him at the thought of blasphemy, and he went back to that kitchen and the old man at the table.

"Fault," he said out loud, like a curse.

He didn't need Vic to be looking at him in that way when it was all old news. Raymond had just been working to put the parts together in a way that would help him through the years that were left. He just wanted to tell his addlepated father the story so that he could stop thinking about it. He wasn't asking for anything of Vic. Not really.

"Addlepated?" Raymond shook his head and laid the cane across his lap. Then he felt around him for the bottle. The white cap was gone. Raymond wiped the rim with his palm and took a long, deep draft. Then he set the bottle up carefully where he'd be able to find it when the moon went past him and the dark was real.

Looking up, he thought the sky was more grey than it had been a few times — or minutes ago, really. And he thought maybe that was a beginning, that it would start to whiten soon. He could smell it. But when he thought about it, he knew he'd likely be able to see better with f . . . s . . snow falling. The light is funny that way, bouncing around in the whiteness — that was something a man knew when he was out in the big weather like this.

"She started out sad, Vic," he had said all those years ago and said it again to counter what had looked to him like a challenge from his father.

And that was true, but it wasn't all of it.

5

THROUGH ALL THAT TALKING, Vic had curled his hands around his coffee cup and let the cigarette burn down to his fingers, sometimes squinting against the smoke, until Raymond put it out for him. Raymond had thought every day that he should stop rolling and lighting them for his father, but in those last days, he needed that Prince Albert smell in the house.

"You know, all said and done, it's hard to live with somebody else's sadness," Raymond had confessed to his father. "Especially if you have to talk around a child."

Vic had seemed to point his chin at that. Or maybe he just raised it to look out the back window. And then all of a sudden he'd spouted a wet string of words that didn't seem to Raymond to be at all connected. A few of them Vic actually had to spit out, pressing his tongue to his teeth and then forcing the wet into the close kitchen air with whatever the words were supposed to be. That's the way he was whenever he was trying to say something he thought really important. In those months, Vic always spoke better when he didn't think. Raymond figured that was why the old man's habitual quotations were usually so clear coming out, even in the last days when he didn't know a damn thing.

But this was earlier, when Vic still seemed to understand, even though he couldn't respond in any meaningful way.

Then, a few weeks later, Vic fell. Climbing up out of that platform rocker, probably pushing himself off his own thighs like he'd always done, it looked like Vic had just toppled straight over. He must have edged that table going down to break his rib and cut his thin skin open like that. But it was probably hitting the floor that shattered his hip. There was no telling when it had happened — or where Raymond, no, David had been all afternoon. But by the time Raymond came back from whatever had seemed so important for him to do that day, Vic was shivering. He'd wet himself sometime during those few hours, but he hurt so bad that Raymond couldn't move him to get him cleaned up before the corpsmen arrived.

Over the years he'd thought about that day a great deal. And it seemed to Raymond that most often people break and pass away when they're alone. Vic had always said that Raymond's mother died during the only span he'd been out of her hospital room in four days. Hadn't been gone more than ten minutes, he said.

"Which means you've always got choices, Ray, even at the end."

That was another of those constants in their life together — Vic speaking up absolute as though there were no distinctions to be made between people or circumstances. Raymond had disappeared for a bit longer than ten minutes that afternoon. In fact, it may have been half the day. He always had to admit that to himself. But David had promised to come straight home from the High School. So Raymond had thought it would be safe to leave Vic alone there.

"A man looks for fault and blame when he needs to."

"All right, old man," Raymond said to the damned darkness. "All right."

Somewhere off in the distance, he picked up a roar he thought must have been the highway. Some eastbound trucker downshifting to make the run down past Lookout Mountain. That was the word — mountain. What had he been thinking all this time? Some other name. Same problem he always had now. Raymond shook his head as he thumped the book on the hard ground beside him, and then he gave a good long howl at the whitened sky. He howled like a coyote, tired of being all alone and needing deep down to declare his whereabouts. There had been wolves here once.

Raymond thought he just might mark his territory to keep the peace, if he could stand up. But he didn't think he could, and he didn't feel much like trying. So he set the cane aside and slid that book back onto his lap. He knew now, full well, that it wasn't called a jordan.

While thinking on Vic, he had watched the half-mourn fade into the grey cloth. Oh, he knew those weren't their regular names either. No more than jordan was right. Or the blew high above him that he had watched all afternoon throwing the leaves bare in the arms of the trees. Or the beth that had stared at him a long while with yellow eyes and suddenly gone away. Or Clara's beautiful blend and the mend at the center of her, where she would let him lay that hand when it wasn't so old. His palm on the dear mend of her center. All these were sounds he just set to what he saw or remembered. He knew they were all changelings, too. And knowing that, he didn't seem to be so bothered by them all of a sudden.

After all, he wasn't talking to anyone else now, and he hadn't in a long time — except that driver a while ago who had laughed at him and called him something that sounded like *sirrah*, taken his money and dropped him at the base of that slope. Just like the note had meant him to.

Raymond put his hand inside his coat and felt the crinkling of the paper folded away in the pocket of his shirt.

"All you need is three." That's what the note had reminded him of, that old slogan the car company used, and what he'd dialed on the telephone and what was written on the back of the blue and orange car that the sirrah man drove to get him.

He knew, just as well by now that he never would talk to anyone again. Not right out loud like he could to the stones. The sirrah was that last one. And because of all that, Raymond understood that not being able to call a thing didn't matter much anymore, hatted here in his great coat between these high, cold-painted rocks. It shouldn't make any difference to him now what the right names might be, not so long as he could run these pated pictures through his mind and make some kind of sense of them, sort them out. The name is not the thing. If he just listened to the changelings before they reached his lips, he could hear that they weren't a clear stream anymore. But they seemed to be something he could make joyous by remembering that they didn't matter, that maybe not talking had a good reason, too. Like God's filled self. And if he thought of them in that way, those names, then maybe he could hear them as some raucous music that sounds like a city. All orange roar and honk with deep *boom ah-wah boom* from those low cars without windows that floated over the street on purple lights. That world he'd seen over these past years alone which seemed so otherworld from the one he'd lived in.

And then he imagined Vic's passable voice rising above all that sound, singing some lonesome tune worth laughing at right out loud for the blue joy of it. He should have started a garden of some kind, he liked colors so much, instead of staying in that house for all that time. Raymond raised his face and felt a crystal of ice fall upon it. A man can paint himself into a still world if he doesn't look far enough ahead, he thought. And when he's been still and alone in that world for long enough, he forgets his own name.

Vic had lost all his words before walking was lost to him. But at the end, when they'd had to give him those pain drugs, what was left of Vic was a cloud, and some unchanged fragments that rose from his pillow in that passable voice. Watching such a thing had made the rest of Raymond's life.

Each day for those five or six months, he would spend the morning with what was left of his father.

"How'd you sleep, Vic?"

"King of infinite space—" the old man would say. Every time.

It was too late to worry about Vic being afraid anymore. On the thin film of the drugs, he'd slipped away, past confusion to a world separate from the one Raymond was talking in, the world around that metal bed — in that old folks' home or whatever you call it now.

He cried every now and then, Vic did, and the nurses told Raymond that his father was talking to people who weren't there. They said they tried to listen in, but couldn't understand a word Vic said. Oh, Raymond had thought then, If Vic's talking to people, they're there all right. And they're probably the people who do understand him.

Vic seemed steady enough — except for those tears. But he was off someplace now, where Raymond couldn't reach him.

And after talking to the nurses, Raymond wasn't sure that Vic was completely safe. That misaligned hip was part of the feeling, and all those bruises that had bloomed inside Vic's elbows and where his turkeyed neck entered those thin gowns they put him in. And so being there became Raymond's obligation and his habit. Sometimes Vic had gone so far away that Raymond thought he'd never come back again, and then it started up that he didn't seem to have any idea who either of them was.

There at the end, when Raymond would enter the room, he'd call out Vic's name, but the old man lying crooked in that metal bed who looked something like Vic had looked wouldn't respond at all. It was as if he was in a crowded room and had heard someone call out somebody else's name. Raymond would put his face in front of his father's then, but Vic would stare right through Raymond's moist eyes, right past his best smile, until some quotation or other would seem to bubble up between them.

"God fulfills himself in many ways, Vic," Raymond would say to him every now and then, knowing it a favorite quote.

Just once, a couple of days before Vic had gone, Raymond had seen in his father's face the words forming up one last time in his shattered mind after Raymond had quoted that quote. And the old man's voice surprised him and made him cry.

"Lest one good custom should corrupt the world," Vic crackled. Clear as day. And Raymond had to sit down. Before that, he'd had no memory of there being more to that line. Vic had always just said the fulfills part, as far as he could remember.

But this time, the words had just pulled one another along the corroded track through a break in the fog.

And after that they couldn't talk anymore at all. And there didn't seem any more to be a reason for Vic's staying around — or for Raymond's being in the room with him. But there was no excuse for his not coming, either. And so he came for the two or three days that were left. It's just that now they were both almost silent when they were together. As though the last words were already said.

Raymond had done all the talking he needed to in the kitchen in those weeks before Vic fell. If there was anything unsaid when all that talk had ended, Raymond figured it needed to stay that way.

"Nothing beside remains," Raymond said out loud to the cold crescent moon, though he had no idea where that came from. You'd think something like that would be a changeling. But it wasn't, so he knew to write it down. Nothing beside remains.

It took a good long while to muscle the pen back into that hand and find his place in the book with the green and pink lines. But he did it.

un bsrm _ u

He shook his head. Best he could do, he thought, and it would have to be enough. So he set the book aside, figuring the writing had become too hard to get right anymore.

Leaning back against the stones, Raymond let himself remember that small waist and golden hair and how she had made him laugh.

"It was hard to live with somebody else's sadness, Vic," he had tried to justify in that kitchen. "That's what caused it all."

But it wasn't really. That wasn't the cause of his life or of Clara's leaving. He knew that. She'd told him, though he hated remembering it because that was just him. That he couldn't do a thing, no matter how hard Clara had tried to make him respond . . . respond to anything. He couldn't raise a hand, wouldn't let himself anger up. And then, when he finally reached out, it was to the wrong woman.

He had wanted Vic to say something reassuring, just one more time — something like "Things happen, son." That's all it would have taken. But Vic didn't say that, couldn't really.

Raymond reached into his coat to clip the pen into his shirt pocket, and that old hand found the crinkling paper again. Hunching up his shoulders to curl the coat open, he worked his hand until he was sure the pen was safe. Then he managed to pinch the paper and pull it out. It was a clean rectangle in his hand, although the paper itself looked old to him, even in the airlight. He noticed that his legs were dusted with white flakes now, and he brushed them off with the blade of folded paper, as far down his thighs as he could reach. That whiteness was why he could see so well, he thought. It caught up the light from somewhere and curled it around the mountain like wind.

Raymond had read once that if something was holding the universe together, man would eventually find it in the light. He didn't remember what the fellow called that something, but it sure seemed to be holding together right now.

Maybe it could all add up.

He knew what had started it all.

Even hurt with the birthing, Clara had tried when he came home from the war. She'd waited and had expectations. But he had put that shell around himself, just like she had. At least Clara tried. She'd rise up from wherever she'd been sitting or turn away from that kitchen window when he came in and kiss him, as brightly as she could. Then, while she began dinner, she'd start talking as though her day had been filled with events, even if she, herself, was empty — which was most days — every day if Ellen hadn't come by. Clara was thin in those days, and Raymond began to understand how little of her was left to him.

Time to time, he had tried to reach out. He really had — slipping up behind her, whispering those old wishes into her thick hair. And sometimes he took her out, to where they could have more of those photos made, the ones that were traces of their best times. He would ask her to tie his necktie, and hope that her hands would end up laced behind his neck. He'd ask her to wear this dress or that one, and she always would. These were the things they had learned to do in the weeks before their marriage, and Raymond thought that they could become a kind of *practice*, like faith — the acts that make two people into a couple. Practice was what let a fellow go forward sometimes, no matter what Vic had said about endurance — practice every day of the things that made a little peace and order, if not quite happiness.

Whenever they were out, Clara would smile for those few photographers who were still doing that kind of work after the war. But they both knew even then that those moments were brittle. And then the photographers just disappeared, and they were all alone in those dark restaurants where there wasn't any music anymore either. Those years after the musicians had left with the photographers and before recordings were piped in to make the mood right again. No matter how they tried, it never seemed that love was enough to make any difference — she probably loved him sadly, shallowly back, but she was too sad to enjoy him, or their being young and still alive after an awful war, being parents with a little house there on Raleigh street. And even though she rarely turned him away, she wasn't hungry for Raymond anymore. It was all this that began to thin them out.

So it happened. Maybe back then he still thought he had a right to be happy.

Without lifting his eyes — he couldn't really raise them just then, or he didn't want to, figuring the face he was making ought to be private — Raymond began to study the unfolding of the note. He saw in the pale wash of airlight that the first fold wasn't tight. It was new and not darkened like the next one. He must have made it that morning so the paper would fit into his per —

penned . . . pocket, he meant to call it. The paper wasn't creased,

but only turned over on itself and kind of crooked, like a blanket.

He stopped working his fingers to watch a flake disappear into

the grey hair on the back of that hand. And then he raised the

soft cup of it to the sky just to see what he could catch in it, and

that fairly took him back to what he'd been trying to admit to

himself, a coincidence, really.

How could he call a word like that when he couldn't call

what was melting on his hand? The mind was too shifty to begin

with, and then it became completely untrustworthy. He'd always

promised himself that he wouldn't let it take him like Vic's had,

and now he knew for sure that it wouldn't.

Raymond folded his fingers into a fist and shook it once in

the air as a joke — who would an old fellow like he was shake

a fist at anyway, so late in the day? Then, all of a sudden, he

realized how quiet the flakes had made it, and he wondered why

he couldn't hear Clara's voice up here. He should have been able

to. He'd been able to see her from time to time, and even smell

her. And he could hear the sounds she made when she moved

around his bedroom and down the hallway, the rustling of her

when she folded those skirts into the front seat of his old car.

That forest Oldsmobile they both had loved and once or twice

had made love in. He could see and hear and call a lot of all that

up in that long white moment between the rocks. But Clara's

voice wasn't as clear up here as Vic's was — or Ellen's.

That woman was so small he could lift her, and when he did, she always laughed — with her mouth open like there were gods to taunt with being happy.

Vic died on a Friday, a couple of weeks before Thanksgiving. And damned if he didn't go without any real last words. Although if there had been any, Raymond probably wouldn't have believed they were Vic's and would have spent the rest of his life trying to figure out who his father's folded mind had called up and quoted last. And — whether he'd found that out or not — he'd have worked just as hard to cipher whether the words meant anything at all. So it was probably just as well that Vic went quietly.

Raymond had gone over there after lunch, like he did most days. It wasn't much harder than staying all day in that house he always figured was empty because he'd made it so. There didn't seem to be as much blame in Vic's sour sickroom as in that long-halled house. Anyway, when he'd entered that room, Vic had seemed somehow all locked up, like he was focussed hard on someplace else. And so Raymond had stayed on through the evening, watching and wondering what this dying was like, thinking once or twice that it had to be an interesting one for a man such as Vic, who thought hard on things, trying to draw one recognition up against another.

It wasn't some sort of staring thing, Vic's being locked down like that. For the most part, his eyes were closed all that evening. It was more a quiet, studied lockdown that he was doing. His wrinkled face seemed serious and considered, and more alive than it had been in months. It's just that his eyes were closed.

And there didn't seem to be any pain in Vic's passing through whatever he was seeing there in his darkness. So Raymond started feeling guilty about being in the room; it was a little like watching somebody who was sure he was alone. And that's a danger, really, even if it is fascinating.

Vic's body would shift slightly, one shoulder rising a little, as if he was working his way through a crowd. But there never was a flinch or a recoil of any sort. And his face danced through puzzles. Once or twice he'd opened his pale eyes, but he didn't see anything in the room and made no sound of response whenever Raymond had talked to him. He'd just stare for a minute and then shut himself away again into that other place. And he seemed to stop breathing altogether when that happened.

The nurses had come in a couple of times and asked if Raymond wanted them to call one of those doctors. But they hadn't argued any when he said no, and they'd agreed that it was probably time, anyway. Nobody — not Raymond, either — had seen it as sad. He'd pretty much lost Vic in the kitchen, and then again when that hip broke and the drugs took over. So it was a quiet night, especially after all the lights had been lowered like they did there after about ten o'clock.

He thought it was about then that he had roused his own voice and spoken to Vic for some silly reason. He guessed that a family of men who admit to reading poetry just have to deal with the fact that high-talking acts are pretty much unavoidable — at least amongst themselves.

Raymond shook his head and pressed his hands beneath his armpits. One of them, he realized, held a crooked square of paper. That satchel should have had some good gloves in it. It's not like the cold night wasn't part of the givens.

This was a good idea, right? To be up here like this, so as not to be like Vic, lost to the world for all those months, confused and embarrassed and smelling like he did?

"Who you asking?" Raymond said out loud and laughed. It was a ponderable how the sound seemed to die so quickly in the falling s . . . stow. But it was as much a shiver as a chuckle. Leastwise stepping this … mountain was an act. He was doing something he could never do for Clara, rise up, do something that makes a damn.

Then Raymond led himself back to Vic's room at that home, the old man lying there and somewhere else at the same time.

It probably had been after that ten o'clock darkening of the rooms, and Raymond might have been asleep for a bit. It felt that way, kind of disoriented — like a demi-world. Is that a word? And at times like that a fellow spends the hours remembering, really. So, out of some kind of circling need, he'd said to the room.

"My name's Raymond, Vic."

Simple as that. And some time later, still studying something, Vic had made a sound like "hmmph" and then expelled a long, sour breath into the room. And that was it.

Raymond had waited in that chair in the corner, until the sun came up and that big black morning nurse had cleared him out with some quiet and understanding words. And Raymond had gone home.

It was a Saturday morning.

David was never around on the weekends, and Raymond had no note from the boy. He probably hadn't been home at all the night before, not that you could ever tell from his bed. And if Raymond ever thought to ask, David surely said he'd slept over at this friend's or another one's and that they hadn't done much, just sat around talking. That kind of thing.

What Raymond did remember was that when he walked in the back door and felt the house that empty, he knew David was as completely lost to him as everybody else. Which was, in some way, all right he supposed.

It's what sons do.

It made the house airy.

And so Raymond had set himself into those empty rooms, set in to claiming them for his own — as a fellow alone, really — which didn't take much more than a first glass of bourbon.

He went first to Clara's closet, eight or nine or ten years closed. He didn't know how long. And he was surprised to find how little of her was left in there. A few dresses that she hadn't worn or had worn too much. Some shoes that were old when she last took them off. There were hat boxes, too, because women had worn hats once, and a few thin belts hanging from a kind of contraption made out of a wooden clothes hanger. He'd put them all into big garbage bags and driven them over to the Goodwill. There had been some boxes filled with writing, too — mostly birthday and Christmas cards, or just the envelopes because she always meant to write down the addresses of these people. Some crayon drawings by David of rabbits and tulips and big skies. There were other envelopes in there, too, which he knew were letters — from someone whose address he didn't recognize. But it didn't matter to him enough to open them. Or it mattered too much. In any case, he'd put the lids back on those boxes and thrown them all out. He'd always thought that was the single thing he'd done over those years that didn't cause him regrets. It felt like the right thing, really, turning his eye away like that, giving her a bit of dignity. Though he figured if those letters had mattered much to her, she wouldn't have left them behind.

And then he'd gone through the house and torn down all the old drapes. He had the D.A.V. come and pick up the over-stuffed chairs and the sofa so that the only furniture left in the house was made of wood. When he'd uncovered the wood floors and hauled all the carpets up to the dump in Adams County, the place seemed harder to him. It was the kind of hard that didn't forgive your stumbling, much less your falling. And if you pushed on it, it was firm. It had taken a couple of weeks to do all that because he did it alone. David was never there to comment on the changes — the brightening of the rooms, the loss of weight there. Such changes wouldn't have been important to the boy anyway, because they were clearly connected to Raymond and to Clara, people he didn't care a whit about in those years.

But when it was done, Raymond was buoyed by it. He slept hard and dreamless for a few nights. But then, one evening, standing at the window where Clara had stood on the day of her first return, Raymond looked side to side at where the drapes that framed her had been. And then he inhaled deeply and loss was all he smelled. By hauling off all the stale cloth and softness of their home, he had also lifted away the scent of Clara.

He was full drunk and inconsolable when he was struck by this. So that became the night when the gates had broken and all the years had run through him. Years when he had told the story of himself into the deep scent of her thick hair. When he had known himself alive because he had smelled the heat that rose from her. Raymond fought his way through the house that night in search of her traces. At the top of his closet he found their extra pillows, and he buried his face in them. But she wasn't there. He stumbled to the bottom of the linen closet and dug down to towels he hadn't used in all the years she'd been gone. He put his face into the dresser drawers she had left so completely empty. He sat in her closet with the door closed, trying to keep himself quiet, as though the smell of her might come from the walls if it didn't know he was there in the dark. He'd even turned back the mattress and searched for her on its underside. And then finally, he found himself on his knees, inhaling from a broken chest inside the rags and cloths and oven gloves he'd brought up from deep in the kitchen drawer. All that foolishness, in tears and the fumes of the bourbon before admitting to himself that he'd thrown away the last trace of his Clara without thinking. And it was that which finally broke him down there in the corner of the kitchen where he'd lost Vic, too — sniveling, wet, ashamed, but needing to let go the shape of himself a great deal more than he needed to hold on to dignity.

"Take me with you," he had said to the walls, the only time he had ever allowed himself such a thing. And even then, he had only let himself whisper it. "Clara, take me with you."

Settled among cold rocks, Raymond remembered that like a muscle memory, remembered smelling his own sour breath and not the trace of her. Remembered keeping his voice to a whisper when he had at last let himself speak to her. He remembered all that even though he wouldn't be able to describe it out loud. Not anymore. Or maybe he remembered it because he didn't have to call it.

And then he remembered what happened next — that he had brought himself up from the floor, his speaking having been nothing against his desperation. And then — it still hurt to recall it — he had gone further. It hadn't been over yet. He'd even been wrong in all that searching. And when that struck him, he had spoken again, calling to Vic once, in the old air of their kitchen, losing control of his voice for one quick moment before it fell back into the quiet he'd worn for all those weeks alone. Where had David been? And then he had let himself fall into Vic's hard chair.

He gathered himself there, put his thoughts in some kind of order, and then broke again. Moving his arms wide out of the way, Raymond began rubbing his face into the wood of the table, hoping that with Clara lost to him, he still could catch some trace of Vic there in the hard surfaces of the house. Some last fog of that Prince Albert smell trapped in the wood of the table where Vic had spent his last days, smoking and hearing Raymond's confessions. Some luster from the oil off his small bird hands. Maybe the vibration of the old man's voice etched in the grain of the tabletop.

Numb drunk and flushed with trying so hard, Raymond had deep-bruised his forehead and his soft nose and one ear against the wood of that real table. Crushed himself purple. And for weeks, he'd looked as though someone had taken a two by four to him, like they should have.

6

WITH HIS HAT PULLED TIGHT AGAINST THE WIND and the dancing flakes, settled into the pale light that surrounded him and maybe held the universe together, Raymond deLeone opened and closed the yellowed paper again and again, like a missal — trying to make that newest fold as insistent and secure as the rest of them seemed to be. The motion of his fingers eased him a little as the memories of that night passed. They didn't fade, of course, but only went by, replaced by these two folding and unfolding hands. Then he started to laugh at the thought that the days of a life like his could address each other, nose to bruised nose, and fess up like two faces of a folded note, all private and creased and black and white. He laughed quietly because there just wasn't enough air left in his chest for a good bark at the moon.

The falling shade had thinned considerably, but the light

still wrapped around him so that he never felt himself to be in darkness. And the quiet of it was consoling, rustled only by the wind occasionally kicking up in the empty arms high over his head. All in all, it was a good place to be waiting. It had enough of the real in it to keep him awake, and enough, he knew, to bring it all to an end in a while, which was the point really, if there was a point to all of this.

"Well there better be," he heard Ellen's rich voice laughing at him from somewhere past. "I mean if this world's not some kind of message, then it is a *colossal* waste of space."

He could hear her just like that. And the "yoo-hoo" she would give to warn him and Clara that she'd entered their house without knocking. That bird call of hers had always lifted his heart from the tabletop shadow their marriage had become. Clara would brighten up, too, when Ellen was around, even after it started — and that's why he'd fooled himself into thinking that she might understand.

Which voices do you hear when you listen in a deep night on top of some cold-lit mountain or another? And which ones do you not? Maybe all of them. Or did he mean none of them? Raymond shook his head a bit and then lifted that water bottle for another drink, all of that trying to clear his mind back up. He could tell his thinking was rising up and turning over like a circle making itself into a ball. Raymond may have been up that slope in those high rocks to lose himself, but he didn't want his thinking to be gone before he was.

The swallows went down colder now and he could feel them hit the base of his stomach, and he wished — he really did — that they'd had the warmth of liquor in them so that he could feel a last swallow spread out to the dense places beneath his eyes and the hard ones back of his ears. Whenever the first inhale of drink reached those tight places, everything had loosened in him, every time. He'd told Vic once that he'd come to understand drink over the years.

"Most men think that at some point," Vic had said to him, with one eye squinted against the Prince Albert.

And then Raymond had explained to his old man that every time a fellow swallows a sip of most liquors, his eyes shut down and his face wrenches all up, just like Vic's was then, to get that swallow past his throat. Then, he said, a fellow's ears ring just a bit, and he might even whoop at getting through it, like a fat man rising out of a cold lake.

"Most liquors put a blade in your mouth, you see."

"And as I recall," Vic had said, "most fellows use it to cut on somebody else."

Vic had quit drink after the last night in the valley. But Raymond never did. It was only that he couldn't put it away like when he was young, when it used to make him amorous. A few years ago it had just begun to make him sleepy. But even though he'd sipped most all his life, he'd never fallen into the hole of it. So it had accompanied him warmly through the blowing of a pretty long life in all directions.

That evening, he had told Vic that was exactly what he meant — that most liquor comes from a bad place and takes you back there with it.

"*Most* liquor," he'd said, "is the devil's work." And Vic had seemed to be relieved to hear that kind of talk from his son, at least for the moment it lasted. Then Raymond told him what it was he'd figured out — from the way that the right drink had always put his mind at ease. The wrong one would have caused harm to him and to Clara, and probably to their David, just like to any man.

"But bourbon's different," he'd told Vic. And he remembered that now, with a faint fondness — remembered that a fellow's body says hello at the first swallow of a good bourbon, or even one that's not so good.

He had always thought God gave men bourbon.

Raising the plastic bottle to his rough old lips, Raymond took another swallow of water and then ran his wet tongue over his teeth. He was warmed with the thought of the illusion of clarity, the kind of clarity you could never seem to articulate when it was important.

Not once, in all those years, had Vic found fault.

Eventually, Raymond had lifted his head from the kitchen table and probably taken himself off to bed. He remembered that most of the next day was gone when he had finally pulled himself off that bare mattress and back to his feet. If David had been in the house, Raymond wouldn't have known it. He seemed to know so little in those days about where that boy was — or what he was like. He couldn't bring himself to. Instead, he had stopped thinking about David by the time the old man died, and he was working hard not to think about himself anymore, either.

So he thought about Vic. What he knew was that his father had become somebody else by the time he died, somebody Raymond didn't know and didn't want to become. Maybe he was just the pure Vic, the man with some other name who'd been what he was long before Raymond had come into his life, the man who had gone away leaving his real name under a rock somewhere in the San Luis Valley. Maybe that's who Vic was becoming again in the mess and pain of those months when he couldn't clean himself or get himself dressed anymore. Maybe that's who Vic was in that last month at home on the night he cut his lip because his toothbrush and his razor had become all the same to him. Maybe by that time, being who Vic was, things like toothbrushes and razors and spoons and writing pens were all just equally unimportant to him, worldly things that were irrelevant to the pure Vic — whatever his name was.

Raymond's thoughts had serried on each other like that after he'd buried Vic, after he thought he'd lost the rich smell of his father. They laid over against each other, then as now, and even on this white hard mountain Raymond was clear enough to see the implications of such a thing.

Whatever he'd been thinking, he had pulled himself up from Clara's bed that next afternoon and carried his body into the shower she never used — except from time to time, to join him.

Shall we go downtown?

His nose and his ear were tender as he washed them, and that was how he first remembered the night before. His head ached dully where his spine pierced that thinking, and so it had been a long shower, the kind a fellow needs from time to time. When he had washed himself full clean, he stepped out and sloppily dried off. Then he cleared a spot in the mirror with the towel and studied his own face, like he always did, realizing again how much he looked like Vic, but only fuller in the cheek. After a long moment, he dragged his fingers through his hair and thought of Clara. And of Ellen. And that was enough of that. He put on his shirt and pants, and walked barefoot back to the kitchen.

He looked for signs of David there and thought maybe the boy had made himself a lunch sometime, before school or after. So Raymond went back to the living room and called out his son's name. He could almost see the sound as it traveled the long hallway and then came back to him. With the carpets and drapes and furniture gone, the house echoed. Just as well, he thought as he turned back to the kitchen to put ice in a glass and wash it with enough bourbon to ease the pain behind his eyes. Maybe he'd been wrong about God.

Raymond reset himself with that first swallow and followed

the sound of the ice ringing in his glass like a bear bell, all the way down that hall. Then he knocked at Vic's room without thinking before pushing open the door. Of course, the smell of Vic was still in there. Why he hadn't known that the night before, he had to put to the drink. Raymond breathed the stale air in a time or two before he stepped inside the room.

Beneath the window at the far wall — the southern one — was Vic's thin bed. Even when he'd lost all other reference, when he couldn't tell the phone from a pair of scissors, for some reason Vic could still make his bed in the morning, leaning carefully over to smooth out that old Indian blanket, steadying himself from time to time with a fist on the mattress, knuckles down. Against the east wall was his writing table and the north one was filled with the bookcases Vic had built to fit between the corner and the door. They were full of the thick and faded books he'd bought at garage sales and library fundraisers for all the years he'd lived in that room. The only other books on those shelves were an old set of *Compton's Encyclopedia* and the thin, black-and-white ones in which he kept his long record of quotations — as if just putting wise words side by side would be telling a whole story somehow. On the west wall were his dresser and the closet. Raymond never did get rid of those clothes — but then there weren't very many. And in the center of the room, angled so the light from the south window would come over Vic's right shoulder, was that old platform rocker he undoubtedly spent most nights in.

Raymond realized that he could see the room so clear in his head because he'd been in it again only a few weeks or hours ago really. Yesterday, or so, when he'd found that note. And that room was the same as when Vic left it, not for any reason like for memory or monument or other delusion. Raymond hadn't left it alone to save the smell of that Prince Albert, either. Not even that. It was just that he never had any cause to change it. Until then, the room didn't make that much difference to him.

But he'd left the door open after that day, so he could glance in from time to time and inhale the fading traces of his father.

With the cool glass still comforting his right hand, Raymond had set himself into Vic's rocker that day, with Vic near a month gone, set himself in between its smooth, hard arms. He smiled to think that sitting there in that way, with the pain loosening behind his eyes, it had felt as though he were encircled by more than the chair. Although even then he wouldn't have been able to call by what. And so he just let himself be there — trying to remember for the first time all that he needed to. Before that moment, Raymond deLeone didn't think it had ever been necessary to compile what he recalled into some kind of good sense to go on. But starting that early evening, he did. Some of Vic's books would make their way to his room — not the marbled notebooks but a couple of the big old library books that gathered all those poems together. Those were the ones Vic read in all the time, making marks here and there in the margins, connecting this poem to that one, scoring wavy lines beneath phrases he probably transferred to his own books once he calculated that they were worth holding on to.

There must have been a method to all that reading and remembering that was just like the mode of Vic's chores. Something about self-sufficiency with some kind of sober God in it. Some sober God of the Juxtaposed. Some —

"Lord," Raymond said out loud to the light, shaking his head in the cold and in the realization that *juxtaposed* was another one of those words that by all rights he shouldn't own anymore. This late in the day, words like that seemed like high-beams through the fog of his head — and he wondered if they were dangerous, what with all the reflection and confusion they always have inside them. But he was proud of them, too, and relieved somehow when they broke through without changing. It was like his stoved head clearing up for a couple of breaths. And here he was, couldn't call a thing he held in his hands.

Then, trying to get back to the thinking he realized he'd lost the word, just that quick. It had been something about the god in that room where Vic had read all night. Where Raymond had been sitting in that rocker, putting into shape what he thought needed to be done.

"Amongst hands," he said out loud from the mountain, trying to imitate Vic's old voice extolling the rite of a good chore, "we could get that done right quick."

Amongst hands. The phone had begun to ring then — which

it almost never did. Maybe it had been David calling in, but that seemed unlikely. And Raymond knew there was no one else worth talking to. Maybe David wasn't worth it either just then, so he'd let the phone ring on. And he sat there making note of how different the ringing sounded now that the house was made hard and empty. The sound was cleaner and harder now, and it somehow no longer had that undertone of the human inside it. It might be more difficult to ignore, but it wasn't so insistent, because it didn't matter now. And it never would again. So when it stopped, the silence rang, too — which from that day on always felt real and pure to Raymond. It was the cease of noise like that could unlock the muscles in a fellow's shoulders.

He reached over then — in that fresh quiet — and set his glass down on the table to his right. And then he pushed himself up off his thighs like Vic, and smiled at himself for doing so. Standing alone there in the middle of that room, he let himself relax, and then he pulled out the hardwood chair and sat back down at the table. His knees popped like rifle shots. After another sip, he put Vic's white tablet in front of him and pulled some sort of pen from the orange-juice can at the corner of the table. Then he switched on the lamp. It was an old, rusted one that Vic had brought with him from the valley for some reason.

Thinking forward, Raymond had known to write in large, block letters and to keep his sentences short and separate from one another.

When he had finished, he hadn't filled up a full page. But reading it over, he thought that it was enough. So he lifted his glass up to shoulder height, took another sip, and set it back down. Then he tore the sheet from that old notebook of Vic's and folded it three times into a tidy rectangle, creasing each fold with his thick nails. In the table drawer, he found a discolored envelope, into which he put that note and all the money in his wallet. It must have been a hundred dollars or more, because Vic had taught him to keep that much on him all the time and he hadn't been out of the house in days. Not since the funeral. Other men he knew went out with almost nothing in their pockets, but Vic thought that walking the street without cash was being irresponsibly optimistic.

"Probably enough, Vic. Don't you think?" Raymond had said out loud to that smoky room. "Or don't you?" Their old joke.

Then he closed the envelope without sealing it and wrote his own name on it.

The question, of course, was where to put it. Studying, Raymond had pulled the biggest of Vic's books from the shelf — a wide book with a red and white spine — and he laid the envelope into it. Then he positioned the book as the first one on the eye-level shelf, to the left of all the others. He picked his drink up again and examined that book for a long while, judging it, judging where it would spend its time. Trying to put its undistinguished title into his head. When he decided that he liked its chances enough — and realized he could change it later, anyway, if he came to a better idea — he drained his bourbon, reveled just a bit in the glow of it, and then turned back to the room.

Vic's old satchel was on the floor between the table and the bed. It was stuffed with manila folders of some kind. They looked to be papers attached to the valley land, which Vic had sold a few years earlier, when it was clear there was no going back. Raymond lifted them all out and laid them neatly into the drawer. Then he slipped the satchel's long leather strap over one shoulder and then his head so that it crossed his chest, and he went quietly out of the room, leaving the door open behind him.

All these years later, Raymond could still feel in the bones of his hands the need to sit down that way and put his life into one order or another. From time to time a man just has to file away what he figures not to need and plan for what he has good reason to expect. It might not have to happen often to any one fellow, but it does have to happen — so he can take some pride in what becomes of him, pride that it wasn't all just happenstance, no matter how helpless he might sometimes have been.

Raymond pulled his knees up and stomped those walking boots against the hard ground about forty or three times, really, to shake the snow off, and then he tried to curl his great coat around his legs and feet again. But it didn't quite reach. He picked the marble pen back up and then the journal, but when he opened the book, he couldn't make any sense of the last thing he'd written in it —

and so he put them both away again and wondered what had happened to that folded piece of paper.

He had failed with Clara, and that failure had weighed him down. But Ellen never wavered. No matter how dark Clara became, Ellen spoke to her with words that were always light and full of air. And maybe it all had been that simple, that he'd been drawn to her easy good humor. It was her way — to offer up some kind of resistance to the serious every time she opened her mouth. She would come in uninvited, throw back the curtains and pour herself a cup of coffee, warm Clara's cup, all the while talking up a storm until she'd managed to pick both of them up.

Sometimes in the summer — in those first two years — he'd come home after work and Ellen would be sitting there bright beside her, showing up whenever Clara needed her to — yoo-hooing at the door and fixing them both something cold to drink, taking her out into the sunshine — letting David play at their feet. He'd walk through that house, calling Clara's name until he spotted them out the kitchen window, sitting in lawn chairs in the sunshine with the top buttons of their blouses undone and their skirts hiked up to tan their thighs. The high-colored cotton of those dresses would swing between their spread legs like pennants on a still day.

"Tanning is just self-preservation," Ellen said on one of those days, her lips suspended above her drink. "White skin attracts bugs."

From the window he would watch them for a while out there, gauging whether Clara was happy enough beside Ellen that he could safely venture into the yard. If her neck was laid against the back of the lawn chair so that the sunlight struck her face, he knew it would probably be all right.

But even if she had already opened herself up to the sky like that, he'd watch the two of them for a little bit. He'd watch how they laid the icy glasses against their pinked skin to cool their brows and their chests and thighs. Ellen had given them those glasses for just that kind of day. Of course he'd compare Clara's soft face, her heavy breast, and her thick hair against the bony airiness of Ellen. She was so small, that woman. And when he realized that he was doing such a thing, comparing them like that, he'd pull away from the window, open a beer, and head out the back door to save himself.

Usually, they didn't hear him coming. But whenever he arrived between them, Clara would raise her cheek for his kiss and Ellen would shift the stream of her words to greet him, to include him.

"Home from the hunt, Ray?" she'd say and then tell him with her eyes the state of Clara and the afternoon and the reasons for her own being there. It was a marvel how much Ellen could speak to him without words — especially since she never stopped talking.

There was never a day that he was not pleased she was there with them.

And then he called, because he couldn't bear Clara's sadness any longer without explaining his life to her, to Ellen. He called and she agreed to meet him for lunch — in one of those downtown restaurants he had taken her to when they first met, when he thought that all he wanted from her was whatever she knew of Clara. Maybe that had never been right.

This time it was Raymond who talked.

"I don't make her happy," he had told her. "Not like you do."

"Well she doesn't have to be my wife," Ellen said, cocking her head just a bit, her sketched brows raised slightly above her brown eyes.

He was quiet for a moment looking at her with a question. And then he had gone into a litany, surprised at all that he'd been thinking about his life with a sad woman he knew he loved, and surprised by his need to talk about it. For their long lunch, he called out all the evenings when he had spent his thin energies trying to cheer Clara up. He repeated for her the things he'd said to complement Clara, the ways he tried to lighten the dark, narrow way she saw her life. He told Ellen how, on some of those days, he had to lift Clara up from the kitchen table or the couch or even from her bed in the afternoon. With one hand on her shoulder and the other spread behind her knees, he turned her on the sheets as on a new axis, moved her gently to the edge, and then pulled her up by the backs of her arms. When he had her standing, sometimes he would lead her and David to the door and out to the car and take them both away to an adventure in town — to Elitch's or the Botanical Gardens. Or he would pack a picnic for them and drive them up for a day somewhere in the mountains. He told her how much David loved the cold rush of those streams up there. Had she ever been? and what did she feel up there? How once he'd driven Clara back to her home in the high plains and walked with her through the wheat fields she said she loved so and along the bank of the South Platte. They'd taken a kite for David to fly. How he'd taken her to shows and to dinners. And how draining it all was because nothing he did ever broke her sadness for more than a few hours. She always thanked him for that in one way or another. But if he left her alone for even a minute then her darkness would come back, likely as not.

He told Ellen that his love seemed to make no difference to Clara, and he knew that was it, really. It was so clear that he had no real effect on Clara's heart. She was unreachable, and she had no way of telling him why.

"It's wearying, Ellen" he said.

And after listening to all those self-centered words, Ellen had leaned over the café table and put the soft, electric back of her fingers against his cheek. He could still remember the heat of that first touch and the confusion he had felt as the sensation tracked down his neck and beneath the tight collar of his shirt. His response on seeing Clara for the first time had been a kind of elation, like a breeze across glaring water. But the sensation of Ellen's touch was more like salvation — as though she could lift him as she had buoyed Clara. And that was why it happened. Because watching Clara had taught him not to resist that kind of promise — taught him that there might be sanctuary in it, even if there was no real deliverance.

And so — because laying his hand onto Ellen's at his own cheek would have proven visible and pathetic and irresistible — he had put that hard urge down and smiled at her as strong and resolute and manful as he could be. Then she took her hand back, and he sipped his drink to quell the heat, at least for that moment. With what could not have been any sort of certainty, he signaled the waiter for their check. Ellen had been quiet for the long minutes before they rose from the table and he held her chair. He remembered even now that such silence had seemed unnatural in her and that, beneath it, his uncertainty had turned into a kind of fear. He supposed he could explain that, if he had to. Or at least he could have before all this trouble.

On Eighteenth Avenue, walking to her apartment, Ellen started up talking again, as though the moment hadn't happened. He had no idea what she said during those long blocks, but he remembered taking her hand inside the door of her apartment house on Pennsylvania Street. And he remembered that she hadn't stopped talking or walking when he touched her, so that before the wave of her words broke, it lifted them upstairs and through her door.

What happened in those rooms was lighter and more innocent than he had ever known such moments to be. It was easy and so filled with itself that it surprised him with its brightness. And he remembered being carried up by the noises Ellen made, which were like bells and so unlike the moans that came from Clara whenever she gave herself to him. He felt sure there could be no real weight to what they did — he and Ellen.

And when she looked up at him and said, "Now how on earth did that happen, Ray?" she had smiled so golden that he was washed with the dangerous kind of certainty that is careless and light. And he was almost ashamed to admit that he hadn't worried it in the days that followed. He was too certain that it wouldn't have made a difference to Clara — that, knowing what Ellen had done for her, she would know how he had needed her, too. He had really thought that then. Ellen made him so much stronger — wasn't it the same as her shoring Clara up through those shadowy days of their marriage? Wasn't it? And wouldn't Clara understand that? Ellen made him sure. And she made Clara laugh and lay her head back in the sunshine and that cool electric-blue sky.

These were pictures in his head. He'd never told them to anyone, not even to Vic, and now he never would. He couldn't call the many names anymore — the parts of her or of the day, much less the reasons. He couldn't, not if everybody in his life had gathered right there in the whitening light, right then, at the end of his cold cotton legs, down by his walking boots.

"Made by the mallet," he said as he always did, because Vic always said it. But now the sound seemed to move only inches from his lips before dying in what he realized looking up was a storm, really. He wouldn't see that blue again, either.

Of course, he started spending Ellen's lunch hours in those rooms and every afternoon that she could get away from work. He began to believe that he wouldn't be able to breathe without seeing her regularly that way. He thought Ellen felt the same, and he marveled at how little it changed her way of being with Clara. She took another job so that she wouldn't have to explain her absences in the middle of the day, or why they couldn't have lunch, but still she came by the house whenever Clara needed her, chirruping her way in the front door. She was as good for Clara as ever, which made him even more certain that everything was all right — that Clara would understand, that it might even be what she wanted.

Hadn't Ellen shown him that the fit of the three of them was right somehow? She could love both of them, she said, and he could do the same if he would let himself. And Raymond chose to believe it — all a great and rangy foolishness that would make him laugh now if he could laugh about the whole of it. What man wouldn't want to fall into a faith like that? Fall into his own Snow White and Rose Red.

"Ah," he said, sharply. That's it — *snow*. It's snowing. So what had he been calling it over this long night? He barked a little. A stupid old man he was, now. And the thought of that pushed him a little toward crying then. But he shook his head hard instead at the damnable loss of all the lost stoneness of words. They used to be separate from each other, words were. Like that — he moved his fingers as though rolling rocks over each other in his open hand, like a magician. But they all just wove themselves together anymore into some kind of — slip solid one-sheet sof . . . his mind fell. To stop himself, he rubbed his great coat back and forth between the thumb and forefinger on that hand and tried to call the word he wanted. But he never did find it. And then he let it go, because he didn't need it to know what he was wanting to call. He could think and watch and hear what wasn't there right now, but the names. . . . He just wished he could hear the things that Ellen would say to make him smile and laugh like she did.

Ellen had a long, white scar on the inside of her leg that he liked to trace and that she liked to have him trace.

"From being a little girl who ran fast into everything," she said when he asked about it, stretching that *raaan* and *faaast* out sweet and foolish like the child she'd probably been.

He could remember that now, her lying there, saying that to him. His asking her, and touching that white line, and then her answering in that way. Lying with her, he had learned that her breasts were small. Not like Clara's. She was thin and light and sometimes he felt as though she'd disappear when they made love in those green rooms. And she would have, he bet, if it hadn't been for those bell sounds she made, sounds that he believed had kept her cleaved to him. *Cleaved* — what a word that is, Raymond thought, and he waved that old hand to clear it away. Whenever he came to Ellen's rooms he had felt himself fall into her again through the first kiss of their day. It was sharp enough a sensation that they met whenever she would allow it and sweet enough that he gave himself to it, every time.

Ellen had those gauze, eyelet curtains on her windows so that the light in her rooms was thin and unreal. And he couldn't resist it — especially on the days that followed Clara's hardest dark shells. Whenever the melancholy rode his wife, Raymond would tuck her tightly into bed if that's what she wanted or walk with her through the night, like she sometimes asked him to do. But either way, the disappointment of his being alone always lasted acid in him until the next midday, when he would greet Ellen as she left her office.

She would smile whenever she found him there, and almost always she spoke through that smile. "We better get in out of the rain," she'd say, no matter what the weather.

And that was the way that she took him in.

7

IT HAD GONE ON SECRETLY for what felt like a long time then but seemed pretty short to him looking back. Maybe it was only weeks or months — although he didn't think so — before he first thought that Clara knew. They didn't talk about it, but he didn't want to deny it either. Sure that she would understand, he wanted to tell her that it didn't have anything to do with them, with him and Clara.

That was the way he thought.

There wasn't anything different in the air when the three of them were together in that long time when the whole of his life was secret. At least there was nothing he let himself see, even with his senses as high as they were. He began to believe that there was no more room for Clara to change just then, no matter what he was doing. And so it couldn't matter. Clara hadn't been so hungry for him since the war, and in those days a man could think of that as justification for just about anything.

So for however long it had taken, Raymond had fooled himself. Or lied, really. Told himself it was a thing a good man could do — hold two women separate like stones without hurting anybody. His nights at home were at least kind and quiet. When she was restless they would slip out of the house, locking the doors behind them so the boy would be safe. It was a different world then. They would walk together for an hour or so through the streets around that long house, not saying much, but just looking for stars if it was clear. Or for someplace where they could see the shadows of the mountains, whenever the city lights bounced off the low clouds. Looking for anything that Clara could believe in enough to let them go back home to bed, without speaking.

She seemed no worse in those days than she had been before. And so he thought he had found the way to stay beside her — thought even that maybe he'd been wrong about what she knew.

Raymond wondered if he could see that long old house from where he was, or from the top of those picture rocks about him. Not that he could climb them. What mountain was this, now? Maybe if he got himself up just a little higher still he could see his home — if it was a clear night, and if there was a light on in the house. He couldn't remember whether he'd turned them all out before calling that number on the paper. Punching all those threes to call the car to take him up there. That's what he had to dial. "All you need is three." He'd heard that. And it was in the note, too — though it had taken a while to cipher out. Once he had, he'd walked to the kitchen phone and found that big old digit on the oversized numbers. David had put those plastic covers on every phone in the house. And he'd held the phone up to his ear and reached out in front of him. He just kept pressing on that number, up and down — 3, 3, 3, 3 — until somebody asked him what he wanted. Just numbers, which he wasn't any good at anymore. Used to be everybody's phone number had an *exchange* to go with it — all of them good strong words like East and Forest and Dexter and Cherry. Now it's just numbers, which he shouldn't complain about since it made dialing so easy when he needed to, like that morning a little bit ago, punching all those threes.

"All you need is threes," he said, over and over, because he could. "All you need is threes." And then he laid down that piece of paper and muscled the pen and the book together onto his lap so that he could write that down, too. After all, whether they could read it or not, he had promised himself.

Ww yvnd s 333s

And then Raymond's wondering came to an end and he saw what he'd done, the only action he'd ever taken before this one here —

He had been holding Ellen at that . . . moment, completely lost, forgetting everything beyond Ellen and their being together that way, everything outside the bell sounds that were circling out from her red mouth. He remembered the two of them reaching forward in that thin light again, safe in the green walls of Ellen's apartment. It was a Thursday, he thought — though he didn't know why that would still be in his mind. His clothes were carefully laid on the chair by the bed. His tie was folded into half its length and then half again, like he always did, and it rested across the crease of his pants. He had his habits, sure.

And all that was visible to him now, all of it was right before him in the glowing mountain night. And within it he could hear the sound of Ellen change. The oh of her was suddenly not a chime. For the first time, it had something bigger in it than feeling, and it was higher. That's how he heard it now, from somewhere inside that light snow. It sang to him a change in his life right there in the cold — high and sudden like it was. He could hear it.

Raymond realized that he couldn't feel his feet anymore.

The sound had surprised him, so that he opened his eyes and saw that Ellen's still glowing face was turned away from him. What he'd heard was her heart opening — yes — but seeing her, he knew she wasn't thinking of him. So he withdrew into the same stillness she had entered, lifted himself away from her.

And when she blinked, her brows gathering slightly, he turned, also, to where she was looking.

There in the doorway, standing straight, was Clara — one arm crossed over her flat belly. That hand grabbing the other elbow. The other hand cupped over the center of her, with a face so lake still that the line between her brows was nearly gone. It had vanished for a moment there, in what he always thought of as the hollow of her brand new certainty. He remembered how she had caught his eye, briefly, and then slipped her gaze to Ellen so that he had studied her face, knowing it was different and wanting to understand how.

When he couldn't look at her any longer, Raymond had closed his eyes tightly to take the blow of consequence. But instead of words or other fires, he heard the breath of Clara's dress and the tick of her flat heels stepping carefully out of the room. Then he felt Ellen slip from beneath his bare leg and out of the bed. When the rustling of her followed his wife into the sitting room, Raymond had fallen off his elbow and onto his back, his eyes still closed. He had wanted just then never to open them again, but just to live in that darkness.

Through the open door, he heard Ellen's voice. She said Clara's name once, more simply than he could have imagined possible just then. There was no question in the sound she made, and no plea. She called to Clara as a simple stone fact. He didn't hear his wife answer, but he heard no doors closing, either. Both of the women were still there, quiet, together in the next room.

Raymond saw that the light was brighter around the picture stones; the moon was shining through a break in the snow sheet above him. He opened his mouth wide and exhaled slowly into the cold mountain air and saw the mark he made on it, and how long that lasted.

"'Spire" he said out loud and drew that same wet air back through his nose, building back to that long ago silence between two women in the next room, remembering how it had expanded so far into endlessness.

It was a silence that Raymond would try for the rest of his life to fill. He had no choice but to try, for the pure reason that he had said nothing at his first, best chance, then and there in Ellen's green rooms, when the silence was still in his reach. Instead, he had lain almost without breathing there in her bed, believing that any word from him would put spark and dust and fume into the air. And probably wrong in that belief. Clara's stillness, Raymond thought again and shook his head.

"Spire and not so still, sigh us."

For all these years he'd thought around and around what he could have done. He could have risen and gone to her, but he was naked. He could have pulled on his pants, but they were so orderly on the chair that he had been strangely afraid of causing some greater disturbance in the rooms. Stupid. He should have dressed and gone to them. He could have dressed and gone to her and touched her.

He could have called her name. Could he have done that from another bed?

He could have tried to tell her why he was there, what it meant and didn't mean. He could have talked to Clara about how it had happened, talked to her about his intentions. He could have told her how he felt so failed and insignificant. He could have explained to her how he and Ellen had spoken about her, how he had convinced himself somehow that his time with Ellen was part of his love for Clara.

Could he ever have done that?

He could at least have told her that a kelson of the Creation is love. That might have meant something then. And he could have stood before her so that she could lift her hand up and strike him hard across the face and the chest and be done with it.

But he hadn't even lifted his head. He'd only lain there as still as he could be, like an animal beneath leaves, sorry but otherwise mindless, trying to hear the sounds from a room he couldn't see, somewhere he was not, some room other than that deep green one that was all washed with thin light.

Raymond raised that old hand and wiped his wet face with it. Somewhere down the mountain slope he thought he heard voices. Somebody hollering. He even thought he heard his name a few times. But he knew that the voices were from people he'd never met. And that wasn't what he wanted. Or he didn't think so. So he didn't holler back. He clinched his lips together instead because there was probably a lot further he needed to go and it had taken so long to get up there on that mountain in the first place.

He opened the journal again and saw that the words he'd written there were wrong. In fact, he knew they weren't words at all, but tracks of the snowbirds his changelings had become.

Undbl You st fos t fin
mebnow _
Im hih throks an they wans eme
Thas wha I wait

Ellen had come back to the green room, stood there beside her bed, and told him in a steady voice that he needed to open his eyes, get dressed, and leave. She said that Clara would be staying with her for a while. Then she had leant over him and kissed him sweetly. God forgive him, he could still remember her small breasts in that moment, visible in the gap of her robe, and the dear, flat, cool place between them. She was so different from his wife. And he remembered suddenly wondering about that.

Ellen left him lying there, his eyes opened now, and she pulled the door to on her way back to Clara. He'd had to crack some kind of thin shell to get up out of that confused bed and begin to dress himself.

All those long years ago.

Raymond never knew how women thought. Not before that day, and less so ever after. It was something Vic hadn't been able to teach him by any laying on of those little hands of his. Maybe that was what Vic was always searching for in those books — some knowing about women, not about Man. There was something laughable about the two old men he and Vic had been. Or were. Two solitary old brooders without a clue but with all those undirected poems fractured up in their heads like dark little flocks.

When Ellen left, Raymond slipped his shirt on and twisted himself into his suit. He pulled on his socks and tied his shoes. They were black wingtips like he always wore back then. Tiny holes swirling like wind. Then he put his folded tie into his jacket pocket and, before opening the door, ran his hands through his hair and breathed in and out a few times, building himself again. Almost from scratch.

Ellen and Clara had watched him, dry-eyed and silent, as he entered the room — and that froze him there for a moment. He got lost in the search for what a fellow is supposed to do at such a moment, wondering why none of the words he'd read and none that were his own would come up. He had no idea what the right thing to say might be, but he was sure it wasn't 'I'm sorry.' He knew already that none of it had anything to do with mercy or forgiveness, or with asking for either one. It wasn't the sort of thing that needed explaining. It was timeless and understandable, and such a clear thing as that didn't need words. So he had stood there, in the middle of that narrow living room, wondering what was expected of him if it wasn't words, and feeling sorry for it all, despite himself.

"Go on home, now," Ellen had said finally. "It'll be all right."

But he couldn't go — not because of any regret or fear or needfulness, but because the lake of Clara held him fast. Her calm was as bestilling to him at that moment as all her bright melancholy had been the first time he'd seen her. He wanted to touch her arm to feel whether she was cold and hard, or warm and steady, or whether she was poised to shiver like water in a glass on a wooden floor. The line between her eyes was back, but it didn't have the high color he wanted to see there, and so he had no idea what she felt — sitting there with her unfaithful friend at her elbow and her shamed husband standing up as straight as he could, a few feet from her, staring at the illegible line between her eyes.

He wanted to feel the surface of Clara, because he couldn't hear her and he couldn't push toward that place in her that he knew had always been just out of his reach. He wanted that reach and that push and he feared he would never be given a chance at it again.

"Go on, Ray," Ellen had said to him. Clara still hadn't said a word, but she finally lifted her eyes with what looked to him like simple curiosity.

Then he'd said her name.

"What do you want to say to me, Raymond? Now that you've done roused yourself?"

He'd started to explain, but Clara had leapt from the couch screaming; the line between her eyes was like a red blade. "Think of *me* out there, Raymond, think of *me!*" and she'd struck him then, once with each hand against the sides of his face. "You do *one* thing in all your goddamned life, and it is *this?*"

"Clara, dear," Ellen said, at first just raising her arm just a bit from her side.

And then his wife broke herself completely against his chest.

"I am real, Raymond!" she yelled, before Ellen wrapped her in arms and pulled her away.

The two women stood together like dancers for a moment, spinning slowly away into the center of that green room, slowly, with Clara's arm outside the tight circle of them, turning until they stopped with Ellen's back to him and Clara facing him over the smaller woman's shoulder. She sobbed once, sharply, with her mouth wide, a strand of Ellen's hair stuck to the corner of her wet mouth.

He could see this and hear this even now, cold as he was, his own mouth open to the snowfall. He could hear Ellen cooing to her, without words, see her holding every part of his wife but that white, round, empty arm. He had watched from where he was until Clara gathered herself and looked at him. Straight into him. Her green eyes. Clara holding tight to Ellen, like a shield between them. Her arm still oddly out.

"You cannot have her," she said to him then, and as though in answer, Ellen spoke her name one more time to end all that.

These were words Raymond remembered well enough. And these were the things he had never told to Vic.

Raymond's eyes focused on the near distance. And after a moment he realized that all the possessions left to him — those that the note had let him bring along — were spread too carelessly around, out here in his last camp. Vic had taught him better than to do that. Some things would sure be lost. And beyond that, it struck him that such an array was probably undignified. So Raymond lifted himself from leaning back and realized how tense his stomach muscles had already been — against the cold or the remembering. He squared himself up until he was balanced just enough to lean this way and that, gathering the pen, the book and the water bottle, and that cane. He pulled them all up beside him, stacked them orderly, and even straightened himself a little bit inside his great coat. Then he shifted backwards, settled his hat, and leaned again into the stow throne of high rocks.

"Thatched," he joked with himself and then almost instantly wondered what that word had been.

That was what had changed for him first when he started having all this trouble. For his whole life, his mind had fairly raced, connecting words and phrases and other rememberings into some kind of picture that he, at least, could understand. Even if no one else ever did. And now all he had was mount — meme . . . moments like that, really, when some sort of spark he couldn't catch would flare up as though his lips were two hot wires he'd brought close together but hadn't been able to connect.

"Spars and spurs," he said.

Upright now, he looked into the pale air and, as well as he could with his eyes stinging, surveyed the ground beyond the rocks to see if anyone was out there, people like Vic had seen. Then, for a long while, he listened for those voices calling his name. But he didn't hear a sound this time. The snow, he thought, would account for that.

Looking down, he saw that all his belongings were orderly, a clean stack of possessions just within reach of his right hand, though he wasn't sure how they got that way. And he saw that he was holding the note again, that familiar piece of paper with the faded lines. He could just see the detail of that in the surrounding airlight. And he could see that the paper wasn't only folded now; it also curled a bit in the same curve that shaped that old hand.

He still couldn't feel his feet.

Raymond never learned what Ellen said to Clara during all those days they were over there alone, before Clara came home to him. He'd wronged her first. This was what he'd always known, what he didn't want to know. When he phoned the apartment, Ellen would answer in that voice they both loved, he and Clara. She'd listen to him for a time, whatever it was that he said to her. She would reassure him where she could, maybe joke with him a little bit. And in every way, she would use that voice to hold him there in the house, when his inclination was to start driving.

But even in those first days he knew better.

So he held the phone to his ear, listening to the air in Ellen's voice, and he waited — got their son off for school, went mindless to work some days, called in sick on others, and waited. Of course David had been too young to ask many questions. He couldn't have been six years old when all that happened. He'd wondered where his mother had got to, of course. Raymond thought he'd handled that pretty well at the time, but looking back now it seemed that David was already closing himself off, keeping himself safe like a fellow does — as if a boy could ever *be* safe, really.

Even as young as he was, the boy probably sensed that something had been done that was wrong and that his father was the prime suspect in that. Fathers always are.

Raymond nodded to himself in the cold. By most measures, wrong was exactly what he had done. But back then he thought there had been a reason for it — even if it wasn't a good reason. It had been all that helplessness he felt in the face of Clara's sadness. Or that's how he'd always explained it to himself. Now he wasn't sure of anything, except that every bit of it was past, some of it for a long time.

What do women say to each other when a man becomes a connection between them? He'd thought a lot about that over the years. When that kind of thing happens, they must be able to see each other's reasons and know firsthand the other's disappointments in him. *Damn us.* They know the weight a man always is. Biding in that house with David, most of Raymond had hoped they didn't talk about that part, Clara and Ellen. Another piece of him, almost as strong, took solace in knowing full well that they did.

It might have been a safe place, between them, Raymond thought. It might have been, if he'd understood either one of them.

Only a few hours had passed. Probably. But the snow had been falling off and on. And snow changes the way land looks from up close, changes all the marks and references a fellow has, so that the way home is quickly blanketed from sight. If he meant to go back down now, he'd have to reorient himself somehow. Any tracks he might have made coming up were gone now. He fisted up those old hands inside the pockets of his great coat at the thought of just how alone he was. Finally. Something was crinkled in one of them. Paper, maybe.

And then he listened for those voices again.

When Clara entered their house that first morning, he was given to understand that something had been settled for now. He'd been standing in the kitchen when the front door opened. Knowing somehow that it was Clara but not certain why she had come back. There were a lot of possibilities at a moment like that. All of them would fill up the emptiness and the quiet. But just about every one would fill it with something hurt or hurtful. So he hadn't gone out to see about the sound at the door. He'd waited for her to find him when she was ready to. After a long moment when she must have been listening to the house, just as he was, a room away, she had gone down the hall and into their bedroom. She closed the door behind her so gently that it hurt his ears. From the kitchen, he could hear the water from the master bath running in the pipes. He heard nothing else for what seemed like an hour. Maybe it wasn't so long. But he'd gone through more than one cup of coffee waiting for her there, and he hadn't been able to sit down until it stopped, that rushing sound, and his shoulders rose up a bit with the fresh silence and the recognition of what might or might not follow. Then he waited again. Waited even longer.

When she finally came into the kitchen, he saw that she had dressed herself carefully, and made herself up a bit. He would always wonder about that. She wore those black cigarette pants he liked and a white, high-collared blouse, open at the neck, and rolled up at the sleeves. Untucked, it hung airy from her breasts in the way he always noticed. And she had on those low cloth shoes she wore on Saturday evenings at home — the deep red ones that made her seem smaller and quieter. Her full hair framed her face as it always did, but that day it seemed to shine more than usual. Standing that way, dressed just so, she was evidence of how strong Ellen was. He'd always imagined that the two of them had done their talking while brushing each other's hair, doing their nails, all those woman intimacies that men marvel at.

Putting his memories of her together, he could see how — in that moment — Clara was stunning. So much so that he remembered the desire that had pulled at his arms when he saw her. And he remembered holding tight to his coffee with one hand and stuffing the other deep in the pocket of his khakis to keep him from making any additional mistake right then.

Clara stood at the door from the dining room, studying his face until he finally had to take his eyes from her — just as he had done that moment in Ellen's bed. She probably realized that, too. He dropped his gaze a moment to the floor by her feet and then turned his whole body away from her. And so they were separate, he and Clara.

When they had been broken apart that way, she walked to the kitchen table, almost silent in those cloth shoes. She sat down there, and he waited, listening but not watching, while she brought herself up to say what she wanted to — or needed to, or what Ellen and she had decided she would say. Which one of those had it been?

"I would like a cup of coffee," she said first with that old formality. Like he was a stranger. It was the way of talking she used when she first came to town — those formal tones that she knew would keep him from inserting himself now without permission. It was as though she was talking to some man on the street who she had no connection to at all. She waited there, straight and resolved, until he'd brought her coffee, with cream and brown sugar, the way she liked it. She didn't move when he put the cup down, but waited until he stepped away from her. Then, as he remembered it, she lifted the cup in both hands and took that first swallow as if it were a sweet brown liquor.

At the sight of her face wincing, he had nearly turned to the cabinet and poured himself a drink — not to join her, but for all the reasons a man would do such a thing at that time of the morning, with a woman at his table, turning away even as she spoke to him. Infinite reasons greater than the heat in any room.

At the sere of that swallow, Clara let herself go just a little. Her eyes grew moist and her shoulders dropped a bit with her head so that she could warm herself above the cup, gathering around it, breathing the dark steam, letting it moisten the soft skin on her cheeks and the lines that marked the corners of her eyes. The deep score of her own lost heat.

All that time watching her seemed endless then and even more so now. It was time stretched out by longing. Raymond smiled at that thought, realizing of a sudden that was why they called it longing, and he was pleased that he could even have a word thought anymore, when his mind seemed to run on colors and light and scent. He wondered how a fellow could think at all that way, without words, really. Was he putting names to any-thing? How many words had he made up on that mountain? How much had he ever heard, really?

While his thoughts curled around the words that made them, he heard Clara's high voice, clear but no more certain than her face had been.

"Tell me who you think we are now, Raymond," she had said to the air in that kitchen.

This was certain. This was what she had said to him. This "tell me." He knew, because the sound of it in his head still took Raymond aback. Even then, he hadn't seen it as the opening to a conversation. And even then it didn't seem like accusation. To Raymond, it was simply, and frighteningly, a task she had set for him. A task he might never complete. And the overwhelming importance of that task had quieted him for a moment — left him a little breathless, standing there so wholly separate from his wife. It had made his eyes search the corners of the room and out that window for a train of words that would mean a thing to either one of them.

Of course, Raymond didn't have any memory at all of what he'd finally said to her, though he was sure he must have said something. Probably he had forgotten the beginning of his answer by the time he'd finished talking. Little wonder he couldn't recall it now. He didn't know how long he'd gone on, either. But he was certain that what had come out of his mouth had been thick and unfolding, because he remembered how it made him feel to talk that way, like talk was a task set by somebody else. He'd felt like a man feels rocked half-up in bed, beside his wife in the middle of a cold night, reaching as far as he can to straighten the sheets and pull the blanket flat over them both and up beneath their chins.

What must he have said to her? Who would they ever be after he had broken through the veil of her steadiness? It had always been thin, her shell. And he knew she was more fragile at that moment than she had ever been. Months later, or not more than days really, she would fall for the first time through the tear he'd made into what took her away from him — again and again. What he said that day had been why later he would take *her* back. Why he would again now. And it had been the second moment when he might have avoided all of it. There in that kitchen, if he'd had the right words, he might have stopped them both from falling — if he'd only been able to tell her who they were.

How could he not remember what he'd said? Even in all this trouble he'd been having, how could he not remember?

The thinned clouds began to take on that iced texture above his head. And deep in the pocket of his coat, the paper in his right hand began to pinch his thin old skin. He couldn't hold heat anymore. Hadn't been able to for years, really, though the bourbon still helped from time to time. Raymond shrugged himself up as tight as he could, pulled his legs up, his knees to the iced sky, pinching the journal against his hipstones. He still never sensed his own body without thinking of hers.

What *would* he have said to Clara then, when she had set

him so great a chore in the emptiness between them? What would any lost man say? Maybe he'd know who he was if he could remember that. Or maybe he always knew. A man usually does, at least as far as a man can know. He rocked his head back against his cap, which lifted his chest and stretched the muscles at the small of his back. Above him, the clouds had a kind of texture, as though they'd been brushed, the way everybody always meant when they said it looked like it was going to snow. But it already had, and they weren't moving.

Isn't it the light that holds things together? What makes things visible makes them cohere. More light than matter. Shaking his head against the cloth and the stone beneath it, Raymond deLeone opened his pinched eyes as wide as he could and wondered all over again.

Would he have told her they were the same two people they'd always been? Would he have tried to convince her that they were still just working to rise up out of two separated shadows? He used to think that way. But it would have been a lie. She knew, even if he didn't, that they couldn't be the same after he'd stepped behind Ellen's flowered dress into that green room. How could he not have known that, too, when he followed her up the stairs and when she turned to look at him through the apartment door? A last chance to turn away.

Would he have told Clara that Ellen gave to him the same love she gave to Clara and that it didn't matter at all to what *they* were? That is what the simple-minded part of a man tries to believe in. . . . Women must think something similar when they need to. Of course, it probably never is true. It doesn't even sound like it could be. But from all the way up there, on old Machebeouf's mountain, if that's where he was, Raymond thought he might have felt exactly that way on that day. And he knew, blood-level sure, that as a young man he had been fool enough to say such a thing right out loud to a woman who needed more than he had.

Machebeouf. The name of a priest with a broken leg. This damned memory of his. If it always worked, then he wouldn't have to be there, between those cold rocks.

"Matchbook," he whispered to the visible air, surprised at the mist of his thoughts and the fish of his lips mouthing such a thing, voiceless.

He would have said that he'd give Ellen up, never see her again, if it would let him hold on to Clara, let them be like it was when they first met. He would have. But it had already been too late for that.

What he did remember was that he'd been desperate enough to keep the words flying out of his sorry fish mouth for as long as he could — long after he could even pretend to be measuring out that task of hers. And he remembered that through it all he could hear something of Vic coming from his own throat. Not so much the things Vic had said to him all his life, but the way the old man spoke, the sounds he made whenever he was driving toward one long-thought conclusion or another that Raymond wasn't inclined to. And when he realized how he sounded — the tone in his voice, the same little noises he'd heard coming from a man who searched old books for meaning, a man who hadn't had a thing to do with women since his wife died Raymond's own lifetime before — when he realized how he sounded, Raymond had pulled up, drawn a few wavering breaths, and fallen hard into a chair at the table where Clara was still trying to listen. As though he was making sense. He remembered that clear enough, that he wasn't listening any longer, but she was. It was clear that she wanted something from him, some kind of answer for what she must have thought a good question. Some reason for what had brought them to such a separation. But there probably never is an answer to a question like that.

When he finally stopped himself talking, Clara had looked at him there, spent in the chair beside her. Then she began to explain — in those formal tones just how she thought it could be arranged for the three of them. And he'd never gotten over that, really. The thought of Clara — with Ellen behind her in that apartment downtown — deciding on some . . . arrangement, some way for them all to be that would pivot on *him*. Some way that was just as sure to separate him out, so that he'd be unconnected to either one of them. Some way that would be threatened, no matter what he did, what he ever did again. That's how he felt, over the months that followed — as though he was standing at the center of one of those metal platforms in the play yards, the ones that go around and around. If he looked at Clara, or at Ellen close by, he could keep his balance. But even glancing to the distance drew him to his knees.

And now, he thought, old and mounted under this ice sky, his life was just the opposite; now it was looking at what was near to him that made Raymond dizzy. Sometimes, he knew, what he could see close up wasn't even there.

Clara had talked to him for a long time, he remembered, talking as though the subject were three other people. She told him he could continue to see Ellen so long as they never mentioned it. She said she'd never ask when he would be home and that she would never call at Ellen's apartment when she didn't know where he was. And then she said she wouldn't answer any questions like that from him either. She wanted distance, she said. She loved Ellen, too. And, she said, she thought his having another woman might make her life easier.

He remembered asking her what that could possibly mean.

And he remembered that Clara answered she wasn't the sort of woman who could spend herself on making a man happy:

"For some reason, Raymond, you think your happiness depends on mine. And that's just too hard." Or some other words that came to that.

She had wrapped herself in her own arms when she said them, but her eyes had been dry — a rare thing for her.

He'd tried to tell her that she had it wrong. It was his *unhap-*piness that depended on hers. But she turned and looked him straight in the eye when she said, "That's just words, Raymond. It's not good sense." He remembered that exactly, could still hear her, really. She said it just like that, and then she rose from the table, put her hand heavy on his shoulder as she passed him by, and then walked quietly, beautifully out of the kitchen and back to their room.

She stayed there the rest of that day and through the evening. He had worked in the yard and the garage all afternoon, unable to keep himself long in the house — hoping that he could reach that private workplace Vic had taught him about. Then he took David out of the house — to the park, as he recalled, and then to the library, where he'd read to the boy, to take them both away. Poems, most likely. He couldn't remember, but it was always poems for the deLeone men. They read and they memorized and called lines out at each other all the time, he and Vic. And still they didn't ever understand a blessed thing — neither one of them.

When evening came, Raymond and David had finally gone home, but the bedroom door was still closed and there was no light beneath it. He'd given the boy some frail excuse and then made dinner for the two of them. The evening passed with Raymond at the kitchen sink and David in front of their new television set. That Motorola console they had then. Of course, there had been more questions from the boy — he remembered that. Soon he'd been able to carry his son to bed and to pull the sheets tightly around him.

And then Raymond had spent the sleepless hours trying to

think it through. He knew all the ribbons that had led him into Ellen's bedroom — they were the same ones that would work on any man, he imagined. The air around her — the bell of her voice — his own conviction that he had some kind of right to be happy. It was the sense that there was no bird . . . door . . . damn, he didn't know what he meant, in making love to her. Or anyway it was all his need, really. Ellen certainly didn't need *him*. Ellen was an element, like wind and water.

"Wind," Raymond whispered and rocked his head a bit so that old hat rubbed back and forth between the stone and his scalp. For a few moments, without lifting his hands to hold on, he moved his head around in the sweet scratch of that old hat.

All that about Ellen was pretty much what he knew — that he had come to her rooms like to liberty, the relief of her. But Raymond had no understanding of why she had opened herself to him there. Or why Clara had come home to him afterwards. He knew it wasn't forgiveness she was harboring, but he couldn't figure out, at first, what else she could be bringing back to their house that day. And when it all boiled down, really, he didn't know who was behind that bedroom door, most likely in his bed. He didn't know whether she was waiting for him in there or whether the door just marked the limits she'd set.

Realizing that the air had grown still, Raymond opened his eyes and saw that it had stopped snowing. But above him was still that grey sheet. "Close to the clouds up here," he thought.

And then it came to him as a sudden wonder that he was bundled up, high in this cold place, looking backward through his own days toward cautions that had plagued him for a life longer than Vic's got to be.

"Sweated through fog," Raymond quoted to the cold-quiet. He heard the slur in that jumble of consonants. But this time he thought he knew where the words had come from, and so he thought of writing them down, just to show whoever came after that he could still remember something specific like that from time to time. If he could find that pen again. But all he had with him anymore, it seemed like, was the poppy in that old hand. Paper. He meant that piece of paper in that old hand. Like a past of that grey sheet over his hand . . . head. The arms of those trees that were older than Vic.

Raymond knew the names were slipping around on him now. He always knew when that happened — and before he was alone up there he'd been embarrassed by it every time, especially when it was so plain to him that David didn't know he knew. Whenever it happened, David treated him like some kind of imbecile.

"Imbecile!" he surprised himself by barking it out loud. The sound of it seemed crisp as it trekked down the slope. So funny to him anymore, a word like that — a long one, too — that hadn't folded itself into another bird.

"Imbecile!" he hollered again. "Imbecile!"

He listened to it roll down from him, bouncing between stone and cloud and wondered if it would reach anybody out there — whether he wanted it to. He knew it was as much David's rusty old anger that made him judge Raymond the way he did. It was probably easier on the boy, too, to judge that way. And maybe in the long scheme it was even fair — turnabout and all.

After all.

Nothing came clear to Raymond in the hours he was kept outside that bedroom door. Or if it did, he couldn't recollect it anymore. But he remembered that at some point he had made a choice — one he never could tick as a wise one, no matter how he tried. Whenever he could think on it at all, the choice he made seemed to be a desperate one. Maybe it prolonged things with Clara. But he didn't even know if that had been a good thing to do. In a few more days, or years really, she left him anyway. By the time David was twelve, she was gone for good. And David wasn't talking to either of them.

Even then, Raymond had understood that nothing he might do would have made a difference in her on that night. And so, somewhere near morning, he chose to accept all of it.

Raymond had made a choice, confused as he was. He had opened the bedroom door and gone in to her. And now it seemed clear that this was the last thing he had ever chosen. The last thing, that is, before a few hours ago — how many years passed — when he stood in that same kitchen, punching one number again and again on that blue telephone.

Raymond stopped his remembering then and lightly squeezed the folded paper in the cup of his hand, holding his heel steady and pulling down on all his curved fingers at once, so that the note cracked at an old crease. He did that again and again, listening to the sound it made, wondering at the color of the paper. For a time, Ellen had folded papers into the shape of cranes while they talked, lying in that wide bed. She'd met a Japanese woman somewhere, a war bride who had taught her how to do that. Ellen wasn't so much proud as she was joyful about them — like a girl when she first learns what beauty is and believes that some light of it is in her, too.

Remembering her hands, Raymond took opposite corners of the paper rectangle in his hand and twisted them toward some off-center middle, imagining it into a flyable shape. David had made airplanes from paper that he would launch from high in that cottonwood tree. When he was still a boy and there were three men in the house.

"Shh," Raymond made the sound of gliding.

In the shaft of light from the hallway when Raymond opened their door, Clara had turned to him — almost immediately, though it seemed deliberate, too, as though she had planned for him to enter. He remembered her eyes, still clear and dry, when he'd expected them to glisten at him. But there wasn't any pain on her just then, only that low anger that never did go away. And in the dim light the line of her sadness had been pale, so that entering the room, and looking into her face, he still didn't know whether she'd been waiting for him.

And so, standing there in his own bedroom doorway, he had waited on *her* — or on the right words. But neither of them had said anything that he could recall. What Raymond remembered was the quiet that had stretched to fill the space between them until, without knowing what else to do, he had begun to undress. Clara had watched him at first, which had embarrassed him. And when she saw him like that she had rolled slowly onto her back — and waited for him in that way. He shut the door then and even now could hear the click of the latch, so clear and gentle in his head. Raymond thought of that moment every time he closed that door over all the years in that house, and then — every time — he'd thought of that same click, more terrible, when she'd closed the door on herself, a few hours before.

Raymond had reached for her as he settled into the bed, in that familiar darkness, and he found that her skin was cool and dry. He raised his hand to her face — feeling for tears most likely. There hadn't been any — not on that night or on any night that followed. She would never have let him see her cry again. He noticed, too, that beneath his fingers her face was smooth. Her perfectly shaped mouth was as it always had been. Her eyes closed only when he touched them and then were still beneath the soft lids, searching for nothing. And the line that centered her brow was more shallow than he remembered.

That's how he thought it was on that one night — shallow,

like clear water.

Calm, she had let him take her — but he hadn't been able to raise the hunger in her. He could tell from watching that she knew how much he wanted to, even needed to. And he understood that it wasn't anger that quieted her — it was that shallow stillness. The stillness that he would always think Ellen had put into her.

There hadn't been much left of the night when he lay down. Raymond deLeone had quietly labored above his lost wife, and then he saw that the blue light of morning had opened the window.

"Take me with you."

Thinking he might have whispered that to the cold mountain air, Raymond opened his eyes to see if anyone was near enough by to answer him. And for the first time since he'd settled in among those high tracked stones, he wished he wasn't so completely alone.

He found his stob . . . his cane . . . wedged beneath that old leg, and feeling the spine of it, considered pushing up onto his feet and taking himself down the slope to where that car had let him off — wait there in the parking lot for someone to come along. Someone who would take him home. With all this trouble he'd been having.

But it was too late for that. And he knew that Clara wasn't wondering where he was. In fact, after that night, when he hovered above her so futile, she never did ask. That was the arrangement.

Raymond laid the cane across his thighs like a rifle and readied himself— though he wasn't quite sure for what — like a man in a hardwood chair set to waiting on his own front porch. It had to be too cold and too late in the night for most mountain creatures, all of them probably holed away like he was. He didn't hear anybody calling out *their* names either.

8

Clara thought she would be fine with the arrangement. Or that's how she acted for a while, smiling when she could, brightening her voice whenever she saw that he had spied the shadows on her. Maybe she knew right from the first that doing what Ellen asked of her wouldn't hold them all together. But she tried hard enough that Raymond figured the blood from her knuckles must be on the record of his life — if time was still keeping such a thing.

But none of Clara's efforts ever took, really. She still rose up from that table when he came home and started talking like she thought wives are supposed to talk. She still saw to David in all the ways that mothers probably do. Raymond didn't know much about that. She made love to him in those weeks — again, like she must have thought wives do, some quiet breathing without any real want. And each time he would feel for the heat between her eyes like he always had and, missing it, would shake his head to himself in the cool darkness. Hers were measured movements. He knew that from the beginning. And she would follow them when they rolled apart with a stillness that threatened to become stone. What had there been for a fellow to do back then, when he had already pushed his wife past the ledge that he knew had always been behind her? When already he had put his hands to her chest and shoved her away from him.

Raymond deLeone had done that.

Then, lost in the arrangement, he had gone to Ellen. In her bed, at least, there was laughter sometimes. Even if there never had been any hint of purpose.

"Shall we go downtown?" Ellen had said and then taken him in a private way no woman had done before.

Shall we?

Ellen never fell into him like Clara once had. Instead, she lined up straight beside him — her face to his, her eyes open and smiling, knowing. That's how it all happened really. His slipping into that knowing part of her. They would lie there still on their backs, their hips touching. And he would vine his arm down hers so that if he rotated his wrist one way his fingers would lie a cat's tail in the hair at the dark center of her. And if he turned it the other way, he could take her hand.

Raymond turned his other hand back and forth on its axis — not the one that had that paper in it, but the one that was always to the side where Ellen and Clara lay. That one. He rotated it, slow as he could, listening to a faint pop somewhere in his arm on each half turn, so that first his empty palm faced that old leg of his and then it faced the dim white sky. As he did that, back and forth, he quieted a bit and lifted his weak eyes to watch David climb higher in that cottonwood tree. After a long while he pointed his old chin up at his son and hollered to him.

"You see Mecca from up there, boy?" That's what he thought he said. "Or just Kansas?"

But there wasn't any promise he could make to his son anymore, not with just a word. So David climbed higher away, day by day, year by year, each limb farther by only a reach, really, but farther still — after Raymond had come home to that note: "I'll call you in a day or two," it said. When David was eight or ten or thirteen his questions would be harder to answer. It was a maintaining, a back and forth, with Clara come and gone and David climbing away and Ellen rationing and smiling and finally saying, "She won't be back this time, Ray," which he already knew.

By the time that happened, the boy had known it, too.

Every moment seems all by itself. Doesn't it? All of them separate like creek stones. And then a fellow finds out about all the things he *causes* in the rock of one moment. Everything he causes swells so big that it clogs up his life and slows it until a fellow is just in it — that life that's not really his any longer. In some sense not really. Then it doesn't matter any more whatever he meant to make of his life, because *cause* just goes on and on like a mud river. It doesn't make a lick of difference that he can call the names of things for a time in the middle of it — between not knowing what he sees and not being able to name it. Even in those few years — when he's a vital man — there aren't any words that stop *cause*. So out of all that, it turns out he's not very old when he first sees life muddied by what could have been. No, he's not. And then he sees that everything hoped for eventually becomes what could have been.

It's mud what isn't mountain.

And sons aren't ever young. After they're children, they're gone. And the ones that come back with their real names are most often angry — disappointed in what their old men have become, or maybe always were, not yet knowing that they too are stacking up whats that might have been.

If he could write all that down and make sense of it, he would.

After Clara was finally gone, Raymond had worked a bit and, for a time, developed a real thirst. He became a man inclined to lift toasts to empty rooms. Not that Ellen ever said a word about it, or at least nothing but "Buy me dinner, sailor?" whenever he needed to soak up the serums he'd swallowed. That was her way.

From the mountain, Raymond saw a glass slip from his hand long ago and spread out on the wood floor of the living room. And he heard Ellen make a small, dear, bell-like sound so that he raised his eyes to her, his hands now on his own thighs. Spending that evening with him, she had spread herself a bit on the couch, a magazine open on her lap. Her legs and her feet were bare, her toes were painted a deep red. He watched as she swung her legs around and slipped into her flats. Rising, she laid her hand across his bare forearm, telling him to stay in the chair, telling him she was still with him, telling him she would take care of it.

"And when I'm done," she said, "you can buy me and David dinner."

Then she kissed him on the mouth once, as if to taste him, and went into the kitchen for whatever she needed to clean up the mess he'd made.

It *had* been Ellen. He was pretty sure of that. He had watched her go, her hips so narrow and her steps small and childlike. The light in the kitchen was so warm that it seemed to rise from her, and the sounds of her hunting around in there were like the making a woman does in every room of her life. Pulling out the knot in his tie, he had turned away from the brightness of her being there and brought his eyes back to the room where glass and liquid shone, even while they marred the floor.

Above that pool and across the room, at the doorway to the hall, he had finally seen that David was watching too. And all these years later he remembered the boy's eyes, hardened and strained from looking too long at what was too nearby. By then, David's eyes had been made to look a long ways into the distance, and locked in the close place that deLeone life had become, his mother's sad lines had begun to form between them. Still — even knowing all that — Raymond had been unable to speak to his son about where they found themselves just then and that endless river of *cause* that a fellow never intends to start. He hadn't been able to say a thing about the shell of himself or the force of that river. Or about Ellen, or where his mother might have gone. Or why she wasn't coming back anymore, why this time it was just too damned late.

Then, with Ellen quieted in the kitchen, the house was suddenly silent. There was nothing but Raymond and David and the broken glass between them.

It might have been the first time that Raymond lost track. David didn't move. And he didn't shy. He was shirtless and barefooted, wearing only the loose shorts he slept in at that in-between age. Beautiful as his mother, he had come to the sound of the crash empty-handed. And then he had seen the type of thing his father caused. Finally, with a sigh, Raymond had raised his palm as if to pool all of them there for a moment and hoping that the motion would awaken the right words in him. A father needs to know what to say. But he hadn't been able to speak at first.

Staring at that open hand, David had breathed shallow through his mouth, until his father had cleared himself up just enough to try to explain.

"She's ineffable," he had said. And, God help him, he had shrugged as though it was the only pronounceable assertion anyone could make about all that their life had become. And he had thought that a half-naked boy that young could understand such a thing, even knowing that his tongue had slurred whatever truth there might have been in it.

The next day, Raymond had called Vic.

And then there were years too many to measure.

9

"Damn it, Dad," that man had said, stepping to the kitchen door from the back hall, in a loud voice all out of patience again. Seemed like this same day. Could it have been?

"What the hell have you been doing in here?" the man had hollered.

It was at any rate morning in that house, and Raymond's old hands were wrapped around a cup. He was sitting at the table where Clara had sat on that first day back. Vic's ashtray was beside the cup, in front of him, but there were no traces of tobacco anywhere, Vic so long gone, so many years before. Books were spread there, too — some of them open. Raymond could see that the pages were stained with what looked like coffee rings and one more faintly with what he figured had once been a splash of whiskey. And he could see Vic's handwriting in the margins. Could still recognize that when so much else was gone.

"That's it, Dad," the man had said, shaking his head. "That's it. We can't let this go anymore." And he'd kept on raving about this and that, screaming really — at Raymond, in his own kitchen — his elbows up like wings as he toed his way around the edge of the room for some reason, trying to keep dry; his every step like some frail thing breaking.

Raymond had lifted one of the books from the table and smelled it, rubbed the page between his finger and thumb, checking for some reason to see if it was damp. He focused on the page then, for a long time, and could almost read the line. A book of poems it looked like. Given time, he figured he could cipher that line out and know what the writer had tried to say.

Doing his best to ignore the man in his kitchen, Raymond had closed the book then and set it down. He laid his hand on the dull grey cloth that covered it, like taking an oath, but it turned out that he couldn't hear anything through his hands. So he pushed himself up from the table and, supporting his old legs first with a hand on the counter and then on the stove, he circled around to the coffeepot by the sink. He refilled his cup, surprised, really, at how steady his hands were just then.

Thinking back, he realized that at every step he or that man took, the floor crunched beneath their feet. Raymond realized, too, that he couldn't taste the coffee. It might as well have been hot water. But he breathed in the steam anyway, and through it, the man in his kitchen looked familiar somehow. Between them was a diamond sea, and they seemed to be standing on it.

"What the hell happened, Dad?" the man had said across waves of china and glass. And then he made an animal noise, almost a roar that sounded like frustration. Maybe it was more like a bellow.

Which gave Raymond time to think about an answer. But in the end he hadn't been able to explain it. There was just too much of the hell that had happened. And so he'd thought about how rivers eventually slide between mountains and pass through lakes and reach the ocean and how maybe it was all as simple as that.

"Damn it, Raymond. Damn it. And look, you've cut your feet."

A fog moved into the house then, and that man began to row across the diamonds, around the edges and toward the middle, his eyes always turned downward, his mouth cursing all the way and calling his father. There seemed to be blood.

"*Damn*," everybody said at once, a choir in the mountains — where choirs should be. Raymond set the empty plastic bottle down and turned to the woman sitting beside him. She was pretty and small, but he knew her name by the smell of her.

"You, Ellen."

"Hello, darling."

"I'm sorry I'm late," he said.

"You're not late, Ray."

"No."

"It's always just today."

"That's right."

He remembered then how easy it all had seemed with her. So easy it was like falling.

"That's the way we liked it, Ray. Open like that."

"That's the way."

"It's what you needed," she said. "Wasn't it."

"I don't know, Ellen."

"After awhile, you were all in a bundle, Ray."

"Hmmm."

"I could see that."

She smiled then, so perfectly, and gave a little shrug with one shoulder. He wanted to lay his hand again on her white skin. How long ago had it been? What had he caused? How much really had been Clara's thick sadness?

"I was just a man," he whispered.

"Oh, darling," she said, and then she laughed like aspen leaves.

"You Ellen."

"We're *all* living under the illusion that we're not God."

Or he thought that's what she said. Not that it mattered anymore. It was good enough that she was sitting there, when he had figured to be alone all the way to the end.

"Come on, sailor," she said then. "You can buy me dinner."

She took his arm with a hand that was still warm and soft

and full. With that young hand, she lifted him up from the rocks and brushed off the back of his great coat. Then she looped herself tight into his elbow and pulled him upright against her, and he remembered how small-breasted she was.

"No need to say a thing to anybody anymore, you know?" she told him.

"No."

"All you need is a walk in the moonlight," she said. "And I'm the girl to walk you."

They stepped together between the narrow passage and away from the waiting place, into the white air around the stones that Raymond had chosen that morning or a few years before.

"You know what would be good right now?" he grinned.

"What, darling."

"Oranges," he said and, bending over at the waist, he swept his arm backwards across the broken horizon of a sloping, snow-covered mountain and ushered her into the white curtain of falling airlight. Ellen laughed in that bright way of hers, pulled herself tightly to his arm again, and looked out over the ridge. That side of him, where her body was and Clara's had been for a while — that side; it was warm and true. And he looked as far as he could. All around them the snow was silver.

He had known what would happen next. That man had swept up the glass sea. And he was angry about it. He had cleaned Raymond's foot where there were a few tiny cuts. And then he had led Raymond into the living room and, with two hands, forced him into that old chair with the marred arms. Then the man had pressed the air before Raymond's chest with his wide palm and said, "You just wait here, Dad. All right?"

Raymond could hear him in the kitchen then, making some long phone calls that sounded raggedy and final. Then he heard the man going back and forth, out the back through the kitchen door — going out and coming in — for a long time, while Raymond waited like he'd been told to. He didn't care at all why that man was doing such a thing. He didn't care because he was remembering those moments when he had been looking the other way through the same wide window that was in front of him now. He was remembering Clara in that sweater, her hair up in that new way. Clara at the center of the room — standing before the window at a still point that Raymond could almost reach by stretching out those old legs.

Eventually, that man stood in that same place Clara had stood and quietly gave Ray the Lion a set of orders that covered many days. He was holding a red-stained kitchen towel, one that Clara had bought.

Ruined now, Raymond had thought, though he wasn't sure what he meant. He tried to puzzle it through, but the man began to speak just then, distracting Raymond with the edge in his voice. And so Raymond had tried to listen, though none of it would ever matter to him. He knew that somehow. When the man was done with the instructions, he threatened to come back at any irregularity and then he declared that only days were left for Raymond at home. That was just the way it was to be, he said. They didn't have any choice. He was sorry.

"It's not safe for you here anymore, Dad," he said, as if that was reassuring.

Raymond had known better than to say anything but "okay" during all that. Anything else would have stretched the ugliness long, and it was already near enough endless. The man thought he didn't know. But he needed Raymond to reassure him anyway, with the sounds a fellow makes when he does understand. So that's what Raymond gave to the man who called him Dad — at least he'd learned to do *that* through all this trouble he'd been having, learned how to give people what they needed from him.

"I'd appreciate it," he said to something.

Then for some reason, the man kissed Raymond on the head and made a kind of exasperated noise. And finally he left Raymond alone, which surprised him really, although it pleased him, too.

After listening to be sure he was safe again, Raymond had gathered his thoughts up for a long wait. It was hard to make good decisions anymore; thinking took time and water. And so he sat there until dark, working to put all of it back together, beginning to remember that there had been a plan of some sort, beginning to remember that he'd thought all of this before.

And along the way of all those slow thoughts, he let Clara know one more time that she should have taken him with her.

When the sun was gone and he realized he was sitting in the dark, still in that old chair, he raised himself up and went to the kitchen. His eyes burned when he flipped on the light, so it took him a while to realize that the room was clean, as if women lived there. But something was wrong with it, too. Raymond walked into the center of the blue floor, wondering about the emptiness he felt there, turning himself slowly around, troubling it. And then he realized that the countertops were clear and empty. His coffeepot was gone. And so were all the other shining shapes that used to fill up the place, shapes that Clara had bought and spread across those flat empty surfaces. He had never used most of them, of course. But they made the kitchen familiar to him, he could see himself move in them sometimes. And now they were all gone, and the plane of the white counters was broken at only one point. By the sink was a red plastic drinking cup beside a low stack of paper plates. Nodding because he understood, Raymond opened the kitchen drawer then — to see what that man had left behind. And Raymond found out he'd stolen everything but the spoons.

"Stir," Raymond said out loud and thought that even when you have nothing you can still have less. There are a lot of enemies out there, he told himself and glanced out the window to the yard they all had hoped would be a safe place for them.

But this time he had to turn away from that pretty quick, and so he leaned back against the sink and troubled again. Eventually he saw that Vic's books were still on the table, even though that glass ashtray was gone. He took the steps to the table, steadying himself by the stove that hadn't worked for weeks. He put his hand on the big grey book he'd held before. And after a long while he picked it up again and brought it to his face, hoping to inhale that old man who was one of the two of them.

"After a time, seems like home just starts to smell like you do," Vic had said to him once. "That's what alone is."

Raymond tucked the book beneath his arm, took up his cane, and set off toward Vic's room.

"You know those cups of coffee Clara and I were always drinking when you got home?" As they walked, Ellen's bright voice was all that kept him warm against the wind, which had been stronger once they'd cleared the rocks and begun to approach the ridge. And he nodded into it, knowing he never had been part of the conversation, really.

"Well, it wasn't just coffee in those cups," she said.

It had seemed that she was always there at the house. And somehow she could make Clara laugh whenever she wanted to — the two of them out there in that yard, in those old golden butterfly chairs, their skirts all hiked up like that, their white thighs to the sun and their blouses open as far as they dared. Ellen's farther than Clara's. He had spent so many minutes in the warm months watching those two women who had each other and had him, too, really. Separate from them, but had nonetheless.

That was the time when either one of them would lie down and hold him, on an afternoon or late at night. And so he had lost himself there, in between them. In the final analysis, all the strength that Vic had tried to put into him failed to hold him upright. Just as he had failed the women he was supposed to love. He'd never really known what to say to either of them. But he'd known that it didn't make a lick of difference. Because, almost thigh to thigh out there in those bright chairs, Clara and Ellen were whole, without him. Standing behind them, he was just a small part of the substantial light in that sunny yard.

"Nope," Ellen brought him back to the whitening ridge, "we put chocolate syrup in there, too."

Raymond laughed at the memory of that. Or was it memory? Wasn't she there with him on that mountain? Didn't she just now say that to him? Smiling like she always had. And so he turned from the ridge and said her name to the icy wind that lifted the skirts of his great coat. But Ellen wasn't there.

Of course she isn't, old man.

Raymond pulled that hat snug against his head and turned his collar up. Shrugging to see through his ice-burnt eyes, he realized he wasn't sure of the way back to the waiting place. Which way had she brought him? The light was still bright and surrounding, but the air was filled with snow again. And through his wind tears he couldn't see much beyond his reach.

"Or what's a heaven," he said and began to stumble his way

into the night fog of it all — he was afraid, but even more he was amused.

"Or What's a meta FOR?" he hollered, laughing this time.

Then he caught his right foot on something, and his left slipped away on the snow so that, all of a sudden, he was lying down and thinking that was as good a place as any.

He quieted himself when he thought he heard someone call his name, even though he knew that no one would be out there on that slope, at least not until morning, when the son would rise and stand there with his hands on his hips, shaking his head at all this trouble. The sight of him like that, a righteous ten-year-old boy who knew full well that some wrong had been done somewhere, made Raymond grimace. Can you see that on an old face like his probably was? He remembered that Vic's last face was on him now. And lying on the ground that way, his breathing pushed against the mountain and raised his body up, again and again until it turned to a cough in his cold lungs.

It had been a long walk down that dark hallway after all that confusion, in the night when that man who must have been David had called it the end. Losing himself like he'd done in that old chair for who knew how much of the night always made Raymond sleepy. But he figured that man David would be back the next day. And sleep between now and then would just be a lost opportunity. It would cost him. So Raymond was shuffling and ticking down the hall, all the way to the back of the house.

Passing David's door, he gave it a sharp slap with his cane. Then he stopped and pounded on it in the kind of fury that had been rising up in him every now and then since he'd been having all this trouble. It didn't make any sense to him, all that anger, when most of this was his own damn fault. But it felt good to spend himself like that anyway.

Hell, he thought, it's the only way an old man can be spent.

And when he was done with that, he lowered his cane to the wooden floor, took the last steps to Vic's room and flipped on the light. When his eyes had adjusted, Raymond turned to the shelves to see where the book in his arm should go, and he saw all the hollows he'd made there by taking books to his bedroom — and to the kitchen, whenever that had happened.

He'd been in that room from time to time over the years since Vic had gone. He remembered that now. And he remembered why. He had come there every few months to update his envelope, to add to his plan, and to make sure he could find it when he needed to.

Now he needed to.

Funny that all that had slipped away from him these months. Or maybe years.

After putting the grey book once more to his nose, trying to smell whichever old man he could, Raymond laid it on Vic's table and lowered himself into that platform rocker. He began to move back and forth there in the rhythms he thought Vic had made.

From all his visits, the room had become familiar to him — much more since he'd lived in the house alone, since that young man David had loaded everything that was his into the old pick-up and driven away. The bedclothes smelled of Raymond's own night sweats. The chair arms fit his hands now. Hell, he could move around in the dark in that room, if he needed to, if it wasn't that he'd always come there to read.

He'd been through Vic's journals over all those years. How many? And for a time he had kept quotations in his head that he'd first read there. Then he must have set Vic's writing aside and gone to the books themselves. But all that reading had fogged up in his memory. He never could call the lines up when he wanted to anymore — not the way Vic had always done. In fact, Raymond couldn't say anything on purpose now.

Why was he there in that chair just then? It would come to him if he didn't chase after it. And so he rocked in Vic's place until he remembered that David was coming back and that there was a package in that room for him. He knew it was there because he'd checked on it so often — though it might have been a life since the last time.

"That's just time," Raymond said to himself.

Outside the window, he could hear cars race by in the night, and he remembered the neighborhood was full of teen-agers again now. Like it had been when David was that age. He and Raymond hadn't had much to do with each other in those years. Seemed like that's how David had wanted it after he'd first seen his father with Ellen — and known from that what the wrong thing had been.

Just for a moment, Raymond thought he had been somebody's father once.

"There's another one of us, Vic," he said to the snow, his teeth beginning to chatter. "Another one that needs airing out."

Maybe it wasn't best just to lie there all alone. Lion all alone. The rocks cut into Raymond's shoulder and he rocked to his left a little to take the pressure off. But there wasn't any relief in that, and his cheek had begun to raw from the wind. It had been good to lie down, but he'd liked it better in the waiting place — out of the wind, leaning back where he could look up into those tree arms. They kept him straight about what was up and what was down. Being on his back like this just hurt and spread him out, and made him lost. Besides, he should be where his belongings were.

His belonging.

He thought he heard his named called out from far away.

Then he thought he heard a sharp breath. He opened his eyes and rolled his head to the side on his stiff neck. Inside, he could hear the bones rubbing together. When his eyes came to focus, he could see the face of an animal through the snow, full and furred and wary. Warm even in this wind. Wanting to know. But this one was large, maybe as tall as a man, large as a lion.

At first Raymond lay still like they said you should do.

Playing dead with his eyes open, which made him want to laugh again. And then he thought that maybe being still was the wrong thing to do. Maybe they said a fellow should make himself big, instead. And so he raised his arms of a sudden, and the animal was gone. Just like that, dropped to all fours and gone into the white sheet of air, without another sound, and without Raymond even calling out to scare him. That must have been it. Become large. And so Raymond rocked himself up and opened his arms wide, and with his great coat pulled open that way the wind began to warm him somehow.

So now Raymond deLeone was large and warm. And the mountain where he'd found himself for some reason was . . . peaceable. He stood up, as straight as an old man can, and turned himself in circles, like all this high up place was his. And he thought, every mountain belongs to one man or other who doesn't have another thing.

And then the turning made him dizzy, and Raymond fell again on that mountain top of his, cracking one knee hard against a snow-covered stone. And that's when he finally cried out, first for pain and then just because the yelling felt good to him. When the sharpness in his knee receded and he caught his breath, he remembered the fear that old men are supposed to have. Fear of just that kind of fall, when their legs break or their hips shatter and somebody puts them under to fix it. And then they're lost forever to the fog.

But maybe Raymond was still whole. Maybe. And anyway,

he knew he should get back to the place he'd made for himself, where all that was left of him waited.

What had brought him out here, anyway?

Ellen.

So he wrapped that old hand around the cane and found his way to his feet again. He imagined that a fellow who was looking forward to any life at all shouldn't put much weight on that knee. But he wasn't. And besides, it was cold enough now that he couldn't really feel it. He calculated that he could hobble along with it — and the cane. So he took a step and looked around him again to figure out the way he should go. But the wind was blowing up the snow and he wasn't sure. And then, all of a sudden that mattered to him.

He hadn't walked for long with Ellen, he thought. It couldn't be too far to the picture stones. And he bet it was uphill — whichever way that was. His arms were all right. He didn't know about his legs. But his ears ached something awful and his lungs burned. Living between Vic and Clara, he'd early on had to give up the smoking. And it wasn't a good burn, if that mattered. He turned around again, all the way around, dragging that bummed leg like the pencil of an old draftsman's compass — his cane the sharp center point. And from that, he tried to figure. Space never had been much of a problem in all this trouble. Generally, he knew where he was. He just didn't always know when. Or what.

It was hard to see through his cold-dry eyes, but in most

directions it looked to Raymond that the earth fell sharp away. And so he walked in the only direction he could, really, the only one where he could see solid ground. Just the same, his steps were small and he could imagine having to walk that way forever. Which wouldn't be so bad.

He put his hand to the windward ear, wishing the note had said gloves. With that one ear sealed that way, he heard himself quote from someplace, "The woods decay, the woods decay," over and over. He buttoned up his coat and set out again, matching his steps to the sound of it in his head.

Every one of them was a labor, and each time he lifted a foot, he clinched his teeth against the cold. One hand was on the cane, the other shielded his ear so that he could hear himself think. He thought his hat was still up there. But even buttoned tight, his great coat flapped around his legs. And distracting him at each step, he heard voices in the wind.

It struck him that they were talking, not singing — and maybe not to him, so that the rhythm of that one line in his head was the only rope he had to follow. If he could keep his steps in time with the sound of it.

So Ray the Lion lowered his eyes to the white, moving ground and gave himself to hoping, if a fellow could call the desire for the last right place any kind of hope.

10

Back and forth in the platform rocker, each movement of air across his thin cheeks had made clearer the memory of that diamond kitchen sea. It was only hours before, after all, or a few weeks, when he had made that sea. And when the memory of it was just clear enough that Raymond could see it, he smiled at the thought and raised his arm without thinking, almost a muscle memory — back with the rocker, down as the creaking old chair moved his body forward. Again and again, he saw himself in the afternoon sunlight that came in through that back window, standing by the cabinet near the sink.

The Raymond in the chair watched that earlier Raymond turn to the shelf of the open cabinet and take out whatever his hand touched — mostly glass. Without a thought, that Raymond threw each glass to the aqua floor. He liked the sound and spray of it, and he liked that there had been no words in his head to describe that sound. It brought nothing to mind. Nothing. And that's what got him doing it, really. That's what got him. Breaking all the glasses, and then all the plates and cups, was nothing. And it felt exactly right to him, sounded exactly right. And the light on the slivers was ocean.

"Go fish," Raymond had said out loud from the chair and pushed himself up off his own thighs, a hand to each, so that he was facing Vic's bookshelf.

"Now."

It was a big book, he remembered, and he thought it was red or white. He studied the wall of them, his eyes moving without his asking them to, like slathering light on the old book spines, stroke by stroke. But he didn't find it that way. Instead his eyes fell out of focus, and for a time he couldn't see a thing that he could match up with his thinking or that he could call out loud.

And then he thought that maybe he was just working in the wrong part of his head. Maybe the part he used was just all muddied up now. Maybe just that part, the part he had come to live in. It *could* be like that, like a fellow not bothering to turn the lights on when he's alone. Or a solitary man leaving his shoes untied. Maybe that's all — just trying to think in the wrong part of his mind, the part that doesn't care what those old eyes see *right now*. The part that has always been in some other time and that used to be the grid by which a fellow could measure what happens — that old, ordered Past that lets a fellow know what to do when he faces something new. Or when the same thing happens again. And when the old part has worked too long, maybe it just clogs itself like the filter on a pump, so tight it almost turns to bone. Maybe it grows into so much matter that it's not a grid at all anymore, but is solid. Yes. Maybe by then it becomes the most solid thing in there. And maybe what it knows becomes the most real just because it's so solid. Raymond knew full well that living in that solid past just makes it too hard to see *right now*.

He thought all of that, and then he thought that maybe his being able to think that way was because he'd already moved over to some other part that was thinner, less bone. He'd like that to be true.

From that spare place he imagined he raised his hand and pointed to that big white book with the red letters on it. And he forced that old hand to take the book from the shelf — first one on the left, at eye level — and splay it out like preachers do a Bible.

It fell open to a thick, yellowed envelope that looked so familiar to him, he nearly cried. Like old men cry, he thought — from the first place not that spare place. Most likely, they cry just because they can't *find* that spare place, or because the bone place is stone sad. Like a cameo.

Raymond chuckled at the word. A woman's word, for Pete's sake.

Old Pete's sake. Old Pete.

He laid the envelope in the center of Vic's desk and put the book back where he found it — which took him longer than he would have liked. Then he sat down, switched on the lamp, and rough-thumbed the envelope open. That made a new raw place on the cradle of his hand.

"All right, now," he said.

What he unfolded from the envelope was a thin stack of papers, a bit worn at the edges. From the way they looked now, it seemed they'd been taken out and worked over and put back in a good number of times over years. Raymond never could leave well enough alone, really. At the center of the folds was a stack of bills. He couldn't tell how many, but they looked like twenty-dollar bills and there was a bunch of them.

The top sheet looked like a map or some such. And it had a big red X on it — off to one side or the other. There were words written here and there along the wavy black lines, but Raymond couldn't make any of them out. Still, he knew it was a map. And he was relieved to know it.

Then there was some kind of list, on another sheet. And Raymond started his work by trying to make out the big word at the top of that sheet. It took a long while, so long that he didn't know if he'd be able to make it through all the words that were spread through that envelope. They looked like dead birds if he let himself think about it instead of making the noises that one letter at a time would let him make. Finally he decided the word was *satchel,* and he thought for a long time more trying to figure exactly what a satchel was. But he couldn't, and so he set the list aside and stopped himself from crying. There didn't seem to be enough time for that. It was late in the nigh. That man David would call in the morning.

There was another sheet in there, too, that was all folded up, and from the color of it, the paper seemed a lot older than the rest. It was an old kind of paper, cut smaller than sheets were anymore. And it had a woman's writing on it. Raymond could tell that. He opened it once and stared at it a while. He smelled it, too. And that made him smile. Then he folded it back and slipped it into the pocket of his shirt. Thinking on that, he opened the drawer in Vic's desk and pulled out a pen. It was his pen, though he didn't know how it got there. He knew it was his because it was green and gold all mixed up like the one he'd always had at work.

He clipped it into that pocket where the note was, knowing it would help keep the folded paper in place there.

Then he turned back to the stack of sheets. He knew the one he was supposed to read first, because it said START at the top, in big, red letters. And staring at the numbered list beneath that word, he recognized the handwriting, even though he couldn't call the words yet — those tall letters and the ones with long tails. The round ones with their slant lines. It wasn't script. It was printing. And he knew that it was his hand had put all of it down.

Raymond breathed a deep breath, trying to ease himself to the work he had left to do. It frightened him, but he thought he had the whole nigh for it. NighT. He lifted his hand and used it open to wipe down his face, like cleaning a windshield of the wetness on the inside come a cold morning. And then he told himself that he could cipher the words if he moved slow enough. He told himself he could, but his heart pumped hard at the thought of that task, and he pounded the table angry at himself until his hand hurt.

"Damn me," he said. And that helped.

He flattened out the papers then and set to figuring every letter, finger by finger, until they added up to words. Line by line. And he was right: it took him the night and near knocked him out. Maybe once or twice it really did.

1) SATCHEL UNDER TABLE

When he'd worked that out, he reached down there to see what a satchel was, and he brought out an old canvas bag with a long handle. It was bulky, but it didn't weigh much. It was a *satchel*, he remembered. He put it on his lap and opened its soft, wide flap. Inside were a strange few items that he couldn't call, but he knew what they were: A plastic bottle of water; and a hat; one of Vic's old journals that hadn't ever been written in; some good walking boots he didn't recognize; some pens. There was also an envelope with another name on it.

DAVID

Raymond dropped the boots on the floor — *made by the*

mallet? — and opened the little envelope. It too was in his own long lost but familiar handwriting, and it turned out that he remembered the note well enough to read almost straight through it the first time:

Dear David,

I'm gone now.

Don't worry or look for me.

This way is better.

Dad

I love you.

He folded the note up and put it back in the envelope called DAVID. Then he laid it down carefully, at the far end of the table, and turned back to the list.

2) LEAVE NOTE ON TABLE.

When he ciphered out what that said, Raymond smiled to himself and set back to work.

The night passed that way, with his old eyes moving letter by letter through his own handwriting. Or writing that once had been his. He found that connecting up that way with the man he had been, a man who could plan and could see forward, a man whose words didn't change on him and fly off — that calmed him some. And by that, he saw that the fear he'd been carrying so often seemed to rise out of the threat of confusion. He was afraid of doing the wrong thing in his own house, and of how dangerous that might be. He'd been afraid to turn on water or to step outside. He'd been afraid of his razor and of knives. He'd been afraid of turning things on, afraid he'd remembered wrong what those things were supposed to do. And from time to time he'd been afraid to answer the door.

Now, at least while he ciphered those words, he had some surety, because he could put some faith in the man he used to be.

Soon enough, the soul was coming up. It was morning. Raymond rubbed his tired eyes and ran his hand through what hair he had. That must be the way a man rubs himself back into what shape he has at this time of day, he thought.

"Enough then," he might have said to the room.

"Old man."

He slipped those hiking boots onto his crooked feet, re-stuffed the envelope with all those papers, and put on Vic's old great coat, sniffing the tobacco scent that hung about the collar. He put on that hat, too — the one from the … *satchel*. And then he took that satchel up, and his cane. He looked around the room for a long while, he thought, listening for Vic. That voice. But the other old man wasn't there. So Raymond shut the light and undertook that long hallway for what he figured was the last time.

The envelope named DAVID settled in the dark, squared against the corner edges of that other old man's table.

In the sting of flying snow, Raymond brought his hands to his cheeks and yelled out like an animal, loud as he could, against the frustration of being spread out over the face of that moment . . . that . . . mountain. He yelled against the fear that he wouldn't get back to where he'd been so careful, where all he had left was still waiting. He yelled out against the white air. But the sound of that yell, the greatest sound of the voice that was left to him, died in the snow only yards from his dry mouth.

With the loss of it, Raymond laughed and then bent over at the middle — to prove his balance, to gather himself from the silliness of hollering that way and then worrying it.

Let him be spread on the face of the mountain. Why else had he come there but for that?

"Nothing beside remains," he reassured himself beneath his stinging breath, though the words didn't quite sound like words to his ear. He lifted his cane from the snow at his feet, pushed himself upright on its spine, and took a few more steps back the way he hoped he'd come. A little higher on the mountain, and through the white dancing sheet of snow, he saw the picture stones only yards ahead, ridged above by bare aspens.

He worked his way there, dragging his damaged leg, and balanced himself to pass between the blocks of pale stone. Once inside, Raymond dropped his body gently down and wedged his back against the flattest rock — where he'd been before. Everything that he'd brought with him was still neatly gathered there, right where he'd left it, and Raymond settled in amongst his gatherings. He was tired now, but he was in place.

By the time he made his way back to the kitchen, checked the satchel, and ordered all the notes and papers into pockets in his clothes — pockets where he hoped he might be able to find them — the daylight had made its way into the house. He filled the plastic cup from the tap. Sipping from it, he looked around the kitchen a last time. From that spare place he had found in his morning head, Raymond tried to think of what else he might need to put in the satchel. But then he couldn't think of what the satchel was supposed to do for him, or where he was to take it, really.

Then he forgot what he had been thinking and lost himself in the cool wet place that the cup made on his lower lip. The kitchen clock ticked over his head, and he let the rhythm of it mark his progress through the morning. His long-peace progress as the sunlight crept through the window.

Until the phone rang. Raymond was so startled that he dropped the cup, and looking down he was surprised that he had been holding it. He wondered how long he had been standing there. And then he thought that the water in the sunlight on the blue floor was beautiful.

But the phone kept ringing, and Raymond knew he was supposed to answer it. David had made that clear to him in more ways than one. So he shuffled to the wall by the door and laid his hand on the aqua telephone that Clara had bought a few weeks before. Or years really.

Even with Raymond so nearby, even with him touching it, the phone still rang and rang, so that he could feel the vibration of sound in his hand, which was pleasant to him. But the blare ringing was not, and so Raymond took hold and raised the phone to his ear, knowing that's what a fellow does when he hears that sound. With the telephone so near, he breathed in deeply, remembering that it used to smell like her perfume.

Someone was saying "Dad? Are you there? Dad? Is everything all right? Dad?" over and over, and that was annoying too. So Raymond gathered his voice to purpose.

"This is Raymond deLeone," he said.

And with that, David's voice set to explaining — on and on — some great and final plan that Raymond didn't have to hear to understand. But he made the right noises, he thought, saying "all right" whenever he should, and "yes" and "okay," and "that's the way" — using words just like that to keep David away. Then, with the man David still talking, Raymond hung the aqua phone back on that wide hook, in its cradle.

He did that because David had brought his mind back to the day, and looking around him had opened again that spare place in his head. And Raymond knew that there was a plan other than his son's. He flattened the instructions out on the kitchen counter then and ran his finger down to item 6.

6) DIAL 333-3333.
SAY:
TAXI
2317 Utica

Raymond ciphered that out again and nodded, knowing that he could say his old address out loud without even thinking. And when he was ready to do that, he picked up the phone. Smiling at his certainty, he began to press the number three, again and again in a rhythm he tried hard to make perfect, maybe the rhythm of his heart, like a Gregorian chant. He'd heard about that somewhere, that the truest chants are sung in the rhythm of the heart. He pressed and pressed until his body rocked with the motion — like a heart, and like love, and like throwing, and like Vic's old chair, down that long hall of theirs, pressed and pressed the number until someone asked Raymond what he wanted.

Against the rock, Raymond knew that it was horribly cold and too late. The great coat wouldn't be enough. And it wasn't light enough for anybody to set out looking for him again. Or anyway, no one was calling — on the side of his mountain, the words were gone like everyone.

The walk with Ellen had just about taken all his strength. That knee would probably throb if a fellow could feel it. And although he didn't seem to care about it much, he couldn't catch his breath. Tucked under his arms inside that coat, his hands were all right, but the note should have said gloves.

He was sleepy really. And he knew somehow what would happen when he went to sleep. Not that that bothered him either. It was a *cause*. And a welcome one. But he wanted something else first. Just one more thing. And so he freed his hands to the cold and shook them back awake as he looked around for the journal and that p . . . . It took about all he had, but he managed the book into his lap, opened it to those lines. They were there someplace, he thought, though his eyes weren't quite that awake anymore. When he'd put the pen into that old hand, he forgot what for. And his eyes closed until somewhere in the darkness he told himself to breathe a bit deeper.

Raymond opened his mouth wide, as wide as he could, and gulped the iced air envelope he lived in. It was sharp and painful, really. But it opened his eyes just enough that he could palm the book flat on what looked to him like a blank sheet. The shape of it set his mind in a line, made a frame for him. He almost knew where he was and he began to lean, to lay his old wish for some kind of order into that frame. The up and down and the back and forth of it was a center. That's what a man needs, some way to set himself straight, some border he can measure from.

And that's what the sheet gave him somehow. The square of it the thing a fellow needs, he thought, a fellow barely able to open his eyes, just about lost in fog.

He rolled that . . . mmmpn across the flat of his thumb and

dropped it to the sheet, his hand somehow welded to it. It turned out that he couldn't move his fingers, really. But he could jerk his arm a little here and there. And that's how he wrote his name.

In cursive.

A fellow can will too, he thought. And then, all of a sudden, like opening the wrong door, Raymond was hot. Dangerous hot, the kind that costs a fellow all his air. Something he'd never felt, like blood rushing to the skin and Clara's blush.

He closed the j . . . and pushed it wide away and raised his open hand to his chest. He couldn't think of anything else but the need to breathe and to let the hot blood out of him. And he worked that old hand to tear open his coat and then his shirt.

There was no tie.

And lifting his balance hand that way, he fell to his side. His hand grabbed his shirt, his paper cheek rubbed the rocks. Above him were the picture stones, the pictures made of rock and light. His cheek roughed until it was nearly bone to rock so that Ray the Lion began at first light —

He had raised his glass to them that night, and their sculpted eyebrows had lifted in answer. Their eyes shaped and wide, their lips dark and smiling at the music and at him. It must have been Miller, waving his arms high at the players, in that pale suit he always wore. Or maybe it was Goodman, or was it before that?

Was it before the war — the pacific? It was enough to remember that it was when the music was the best thing in their night, in their lives just then. And to remember that it lasted all through that rare evening.

They were dancing. Ellen and Clara. Together at first, cheek to cheek. They danced close, and dark, without him, though they both looked his way from time to time and laughed. It was something that burst out of them, that laugh. Like women. And when he raised his glass to it, they rocked their heads back so that their hair fell behind them and then they spun out across the dark shining floor. The lights turned, too, and the music was somewhere behind him — and inside of him, like the scent of mountain air. And he raised his glass again, smiling, but silent to the notes around him, and watching the two of them together like that. They turned and they turned, for just that night open to everything, beneath the lights and inside the music. And he could hear their voices chiming with the sweet horns and ringing clarinets. And their mouths were white and red and laughing, lit as they danced. And as they turned, Clara's arm was strangely outstretched reaching toward him, wondering, and laughing at what Ellen had whispered to her.

And that night, Raymond was the fellow an arm's length away.

11

For some long minutes before noon, Raymond had ridden in that orange and blue car out of the city, and a long way through the foothills. He thought that driver was talking to him, but he didn't understand a word the man said. Out the window, the signs and the words went by him and then were gone and all he could see was stone and trees. The moments.

He'd always loved these mo . . . these mountains. They took the heat off a fellow. And it was a good morning for a ride.

"Isn't it?"

But he might not have said that out loud. It was hard to tell.

When they'd passed the first range, he could see snow on the peaks in the distance. Most years it was there no matter what the season. But he thought it was fall now. He was falling, the snow was. And so the worst of the heat was over for the year. And the air through the cracked window was cool. A blush.

The driver held up the paper Raymond had given him. It looked like a map, like a treasure map, really, with a red X, off center. The place they were supposed to go in that orange car. And blue.

He asked something that Raymond didn't understand, and so he just said

"I'm sure."

Or thought he did. The driver made some angry sound at that, and Raymond turned to look out the window again, pleased by all this moving. He had somewhere that he was supposed to be, and the driver would know where that was. You just give them the address and they go there.

Something bulky was pushing against Raymond's back, and he pulled it around in front of him to see what it was. If you stare long enough, sometimes it works its way through you and you know what it is, even if you still can't call it.

He knew what it was then. He was supposed to carry it up from where the car would stop.

They used to picnic up there somewhere, he thought. And then leaned forward as the car slowed and left the highway. His forehead almost touched that place in front of him, and then he bounced back against the seat, that bulk behind him again.

He made some kind of noise that he didn't think was proper, and then the car turned this way and that, like it was lost.

The driver held the paper in one hand on the wheel and kept looking from side to side. Raymond nodded at that because he knew that the man was working and that things were moving forward.

Then he heard the crunch of glass — or rocks — under the car, the orange and blue car, and the driver brought them to be still. He looked over his shoulder at Raymond — laying his arm along the soft wall between them, where Raymond had almost hit his head. And he talked for a while. Raymond was sure it was good advice, and so he reached into his great coat pocket and pulled out the money he had brought with him. It had once been folded up in that sheet that looked like a map.

But when he looked back up, the man was gone. And then the door beside Raymond opened.

"Oh," he said.

A hand took his arm, lifted him out of the car, and pulled him up to standing. Then the man handed Raymond his cane. Raymond thanked him, listened a little more to what the man had to say, and then gave him all that money.

He turned away then and looked at the place he was to go. The rock trail led into the trees, and he knew that once he was behind them, the trail would go up. So he raised his eyes, but couldn't see that far, really. Behind him, he heard the door shut. And then he heard the car leave. When he finally turned back to see, he was alone and there was dust in the air.

Clara and David wouldn't know where to look.

Raymond patted all his pockets, because that's what a man does before setting out. It was all in order as far as he could tell. He didn't carry much with him anymore, really. His pen was in his pocket, which wasn't where he ever kept it. But it was there. And when he patted it, the pocket crunched a little beneath his palm. Something behind that pen. Something like a piece of paper. It took awhile for him to fish it out. But he did. And he knew what it was from the lines and the shape of it. That old passage. With his cane crooked on his arm he unfolded it slowly in the grey morning light. An old slip like that could tear pretty easily.

He couldn't read it with those old eyes, but he knew what it said. He must have read it a million times before.

Dear Ray,

She won't be back this time. You could see that in her, too. Don't think too much about it, or you'll miss everything else.

You should lose yourself in life, Ray.

I'll be lost in it, too —someplace,

Ellen

That's what it said, he nodded, folding the paper back up. It said that, because Raymond had spent his life like Vic, and they remembered the important words. The old men he was.

That's what she wrote. That someplace Ellen.

Raymond regained the folds and slipped the paper back into his pocket, pushed it under that good pen. It was a good pen that he'd had for hours, or years, really. And then he patted them both with his open palm, losing himself a little in the rhythm of that. Some new sound behind him, some mountain sound, brought Raymond still again. And so he settled the paper and gathered himself and buttoned Vic's great coat all up straight. He bounced a little to set the bulk of the satchel to ride right on his hip. Then he leaned hard on his cane, tested it, turned himself again, and walked to the trees. Those were good boots. Behind him now was the shush of cars. But he could hear the wind quaking the leaves over his head. *Aspens* he thought and was proud to know that still. That man, David, thought he didn't know.

And he and Clara didn't know where to look.

Just inside the first curtain of trees, Raymond shrugged and closed his eyes a minute to listen before he set to walking. He was surprised at how good that felt, to rest them that way.

He smelled the air — like cars and dust and vanilla pines and cold all at once, up high in snow-topped mountains and so far from that house.

He heard the sounds of the road behind him, and he breathed into the climb he still had to make. His hands, he thought, were like sleeping birds: one in his pocket, the other balanced on his cane, where it had been for years. And though he couldn't quite call the name for it, he understood that all of him was right there. Even the land seemed familiar to him, and he sighed easily into that. Then Raymond deLeone took the first few steps up the trail. Each pull was hard on his legs. But what brought him up short was the thought of that house, and his brow wrinkled up just a bit — wondering whether he'd remembered to close the door.

Nov__ sun 2 0 - DAY

Undbl You st fos t fin
mebnow __
Im hih throks an they wans eme
Thas wha I wait
yse an Im not lost
last rly
Im not last.
Hre 1 ctch s pel
dfl fs slf umumn ys
Iv scaaa rt of thphy
un bsrm _ n
Ww yund s 333s

aRym ViL_la (on_

About the Author

Frederick Ramey is an editor of literary fiction and memoir. He is also co-publisher of Unbridled Books and the founding director of Leaping Man, a not-for-profit producer of performances, arguments, & artifacts in Colorado. You can find him at leapingman.org.

Fomite

About Fomite

A fomite is a medium capable of transmitting infectious organisms from one indi-vidual to another.

"The activity of art is based on the capacity of people to be infected by the feelings of others." Tolstoy, *What Is Art?*

Writing a review on Amazon, Good Reads, Shelfari, Library Thing or other social media sites for readers will help the progress of independent publishing. To submit a review, go to the book page on any of the sites and follow the links for reviews. Books from independent presses rely on reader to reader communications.

For more information or to order any of our books, visit
https://www.fomitepress.com/our-books.html

More Titles from Fomite...

Novels
Joshua Amses — *During This, Our Nadir*
Joshua Amses — *Ghatsr*
Joshua Amses — *Raven or Crow*
Joshua Amses — *The Moment Before an Injury*
Jaysinh Birjepatel — *Nothing Beside Remains*
Jaysinh Birjepatel — *The Good Muslim of Jackson Heights*
David Brizer — *Victor Rand*
Paula Closson Buck — *Summer on the Cold War Planet*
Dan Chodorkoff — *Loisaida*
David Adams Cleveland — *Time's Betrayal*
Jaimee Wriston Colbert — *Vanishing Acts*
Roger Coleman — *Skywreck Afternoons*
Marc Estrin — *Hyde*
Marc Estrin — *Kafka's Roach*
Marc Estrin — *Speckled Vanities*
Zdravka Evtimova — *In the Town of Joy and Peace*
Zdravka Evtimova — *Sinfonia Bulgarica*
Daniel Forbes — *Derail This Train Wreck*
Greg Guma — *Dons of Time*
Richard Hawley — *The Three Lives of Jonathan Force*

Fomite

Fomite

Peter M. Wheelwright — *As It Is On Earth*

Suzie Wizowaty — *The Return of Jason Green*

Poetry

Anna Blackmer — *Hexagrams*

Antonello Borra — *Alfabestiario*

Antonello Borra — *AlphaBetaBestiaro*

Antonello Borra — *The Factory of Ideas*

L. Brown — *Loopholes*

Sue D. Burton — *Little Steel*

David Cavanagh— *Cycling in Plato's Cave*

James Connolly — *Picking Up the Bodies*

Greg Delanty — *Loosestrife*

Mason Drukman — *Drawing on Life*

J. C. Ellefson — *Foreign Tales of Exemplum and Woe*

Tina Escaja/Mark Eisner — *Caida Libre/Free Fall*

Anna Faktorovich — *Improvisational Arguments*

Barry Goldensohn — *Snake in the Spine, Wolf in the Heart*

Barry Goldensohn — *The Hundred Yard Dash Man*

Barry Goldensohn — *The Listener Aspires to the Condition of Music*

R. L. Green — *When You Remember Deir Yassin*

Gail Holst-Warhaft — *Lucky Country*

Raymond Luczak — *A Babble of Objects*

Kate Magill — *Roadworthy Creature, Roadworthy Craft*

Tony Magistrale — *Entanglements*

Gary Mesick — *General Discharge*

Andreas Nolte — *Mascha: The Poems of Mascha Kaléko*

Sherry Olson — *Four-Way Stop*

Brett Ortler — *Lessons of the Dead*

Aristea Papalexandrou/Philip Ramp — *Μας προσπερνά/It's Overtaking Us*

Janice Miller Potter — *Meanwell*

Janice Miller Potter — *Thoreau's Umbrella*

Philip Ramp — *The Melancholy of a Life as the Joy of Living It Slowly Chills*

Joseph D. Reich — *A Case Study of Werewolves*

Joseph D. Reich — *Connecting the Dots to Shangrila*

Joseph D. Reich — *The Derivation of Cowboys and Indians*

Joseph D. Reich — *The Hole That Runs Through Utopia*

Joseph D. Reich — *The Housing Market*

Kenneth Rosen and Richard Wilson — *Gomorrah*

Fomite

Fred Rosenblum — *Vietnumb*

David Schein — *My Murder and Other Local News*

Harold Schweizer — *Miriam's Book*

Scott T. Starbuck — *Carbonfish Blues*

Scott T. Starbuck — *Hawk on Wire*

Scott T. Starbuck — *Industrial Oz*

Seth Steinzor — *Among the Lost*

Seth Steinzor — *To Join the Lost*

Susan Thomas — *In the Sadness Museum*

Susan Thomas — *The Empty Notebook Interrogates Itself*

Paolo Valesio/Todd Portnowitz — *La Mezzanotte di Spoleto/Midnight in Spoleto*

Sharon Webster — *Everyone Lives Here*

Tony Whedon — *The Tres Riches Heures*

Tony Whedon — *The Falkland Quartet*

Claire Zoghb — *Dispatches from Everest*

Stories

Jay Boyer — *Flight*

MaryEllen Beveridge — *After the Hunger*

L. M Brown — *Treading the Uneven Road*

Michael Cocchiarale — *Here Is Ware*

Michael Cocchiarale — *Still Time*

Neil Connelly — *In the Wake of Our Vows*

Catherine Zobal Dent — *Unfinished Stories of Girls*

Zdravka Evtimova —*Carts and Other Stories*

John Michael Flynn — *Off to the Next Wherever*

Derek Furr — *Semitones*

Derek Furr — *Suite for Three Voices*

Elizabeth Genovise — *Where There Are Two or More*

Andrei Guriuanu — *Body of Work*

Zeke Jarvis — *In A Family Way*

Arya Jenkins — *Blue Songs in an Open Key*

Jan English Leary — *Skating on the Vertical*

Marjorie Maddox — *What She Was Saying*

William Marquess — *Boom-shacka-lacka*

Gary Miller — *Museum of the Americas*

Jennifer Anne Moses — *Visiting Hours*

Martin Ott — *Interrogations*

Christopher S. Peterson — *Amoebic Simulacra*

Fomite

Odd Birds

Plays

Essays

9 781944 388720